CHAPTER

Under a noon sun the vast, flat country, buried deep in snow, lay like a paper hoop rimmed by the dark primeval forest; its surface shone with an unbearable brightness as of sun-struck glass, every crystal gleaming and quivering with intense cold light. To the north a single blunt, low mountain-head broke the evenness of the horizon line.

Hugh Garth seemed to leap through paper like a tiny active clown as he dropped down into the small space shoveled clear in front of his hidden cabin door. The roof was weighted with drift, so that a curling mass like the edge of a wind-crowded wave about to break hung low over the eaves. Long icicles as thick as a man's arm stretched from roof to ground in a row of twisted columns. Under this overhanging cornice of snow near the door there was a sudden icy purple darkness.

As Hugh plunged down into it, his face lost a certain rapt brightness and shadowed deeply. He let slip the load of fresh pelts from his back, drew his feet from the skis which he stuck up on their ends in the snow, and removed the fur cap from his head and the huge dark spectacles from his eyes. Then, crouching, he went in at the low, ill-hung door. It stuck to its sill, and he cursed it; all his movements expressed the anger of frustration. He slammed the door behind him.

Buried in drifts, the cabin was dim even at this bright hour of noon. The stove glowed in a corner with a subdued redness, its bulging cheeks and round mouth dully scarlet. The low room was pleasant to look at, for it had the beauty of brown bark and the salmon tints of old rough boards, and its furniture, wrought painstakingly by an unskillful hand, had the charm of all handwork even when unskilled. Some of the chairs were rudely carved, one great throne especially, awkward, pretentious, and carefully ornate.

There was, too, a solid table in the center of the floor; and on it a woman was setting heavy earthenware plates nicked and discolored. She was heavy and discolored herself, but like the stove, she too seemed to have a dull glow. She was no longer young, but she might still have encouraged her youthfulness to linger pleasantly; she was not in the least degree beautiful, but she might have fostered a charm that lurked somewhere about her small, compact body and in her square, dark face. Her hair of a sandy brown was stretched back brutally so that her bright, devoted eyes—gray and honest eyes, very deep-set beneath their brows—lacked the usual softness and mystery of women's eyes. Her lips were tight set; her chin held out with an air of dogged effort which seemed to possess no relation to her mechanical occupation, yet to have a strong habitual relation to her state of mind. She seemed, in fact, under a shell of self-control, to conceal an inner light, like a dimly burning dark-lantern. Her expression was dumb. She moved about like a deaf-mute. Indeed, her stillness and stony self-repression were extraordinary.

A youth rose from a chair near the stove and greeted Hugh as he entered.

"Hullo," he said. "How many did you get?"

It was the eager questioning of a modest, affectionate boy who curbs his natural effervescence of greeting like a well-trained dog. The tone was astonishingly young, a quiet, husky boy-voice.

"Damn you, Pete!" was snarled at him for answer. "Haven't you got my boot mended yet?"

The boot, still lacking its heel, lay on the floor near the stove, and Hugh now picked it up and hurled it half across the room.

"I have to get out into this ice chest of a wilderness and this flaming glare that cuts my eyeballs open, and work till the sweat freezes on my face, and then come home to find you loafing by the fire as if you were a house cat—purring and rubbing against my legs when I come in," he snarled. "Thanking me for a quiet nap and a saucer of milk, eh? You loafer! What do I keep you for? You gorge the bread and meat I earn by sweating and freezing, and you keep your sluggish mountain of bones covered. A year or two ago I'd have urged you along with a stick. I used to get some work out of you then. But you think you're too big for that, now, don't you? You fancy I'm afraid of your bigness, eh? Well, do you want me to try it out? What about it?"

During the first part of his brother's speech, Pete had faced him, but in the middle he had turned his back and stood in front of one of the clumsy windows. He looked out now at a white wall of snow, above which shone the dazzle of the midday. He whistled very softly to himself and sank his hands deep into the pockets of his corduroys. He did not answer the snarling question, but his wide, quiet mouth, exquisitely shaped, ran into a smile and a dimple, deep and narrow, cut into his thin and ruddy cheek.

Between the woman, who went on with her work as though no one had come into the room, and the silent smiling youth, Hugh Garth prowled the floor like a shadow thrown by a moving light.

He was a man of forty-five, gray-haired, misshapen, heavy above the waist and light to meanness below; a man lame in one leg and with an ill-proportioned face, malicious, lined, lead-colored; a man who limped and leaped about the room with a fierce energy, the while his tongue, gifted with a rich and resonant voice, poured vitriol upon the silence.

Suddenly the woman spoke. She turned back on the threshold of the kitchen door through which her work had been taking her to and fro during Garth's outbreak. Her voice was monotonous and smothered; it had its share in her unnatural self-repression.

"Why don't you tell him to be quiet, Pete? You've been chopping wood since daybreak to make up for what he didn't do last week, and you only came in about ten minutes before he did. Why don't you speak out? You're getting to be pretty close to a man now, and it isn't suitable for you to let yourself be talked to that way. You always stand like a fool and take it from him."

Pete turned. "Oh, well," he answered good-humoredly, "I guess maybe he's tired. Let up, Hugh, will you? I'll finish your boot after dinner."

"The hell you will! You'll do it now!" Venting on his brother his anger at the woman's intervention, Garth swung his misshapen body around the end of the table and thrust an elbow violently against Pete's chest. The attack was so unexpected that Pete staggered, lost his balance, and stepping down into the shallow depression of a pebbled hearth, fell, twisting his ankle. The agony was sharp. After a dumb minute he lifted a white face and pulled himself up, one hand clutching the board mantel. "Now you've done it!" he said between his teeth. "How will you get your pelts to the station now? I won't be able to take them."

There ensued a dismayed silence. The woman had come back from the kitchen and stood with a steaming dish in her hands. After the brief pause of consternation she set down the dish and went over to Pete. "Here," she said, "sit down and let me take off your moccasin and bathe your ankle before it begins to swell."

Hugh Garth had seated himself in the thronelike chair at the head of the table. His expression was still defiant, indifferent, and lordly. "Come and eat your dinner, both of you," he commanded. "You've had your lesson, Pete. After this, I guess you'll do what I tell you to—not choose the work that happens to suit your humor. Don't, for God's sake, baby him, Bella. Don't start being a grandmother before you've ever been a sweetheart. You're too young for the one even if you're getting a bit too old for the other!"

Bella flushed deep and hot. She went to her place, and Pete hobbled to his, opposite his brother. Between them the woman sat, dyed deep in her sudden unaccustomed wave of scarlet. Pete's whiteness too was stained in sympathy. But Hugh only chuckled. "As for the pelts," he said royally, "I'll take them down myself."

Bella looked slowly up.

"You think I don't mean it, I suppose?" Hugh demanded.

They did not answer, but the eyes of the boy and the woman met. This silence and this dumb exchange of understanding infuriated Garth. He clinched his hands on the carved arms of his chair and leaned a little forward.

"I'll take the pelts myself," he repeated boisterously. "I'm not afraid to be seen at the station. I'm sick of skulking. Buried here—with *my* talents—in this damn country, spending my days trapping and skinning beasts to keep the breath in our three useless bodies. Wouldn't death be better for a man like me? Easier to bear? Fifteen years of it! Fifteen years! My best years!" He stared over Pete's head. "In all that time no beauty to feed my starved senses, no work for my starved brain, no hope for my starved heart." The woman and the youth watched him still in silence. "That fox I killed this morning had a better life to lose than I."

"It wouldn't be safe for you to go, Hugh," said Pete gently.

"Why not—watchdog?"

The sneer deepened the flush on Pete's face, but he answered with the same gentleness, fixing his blue eyes on his brother's.

"Because not two months ago there was a picture of you tacked up in the post-office."

Bella's face whitened, and Hugh's cheeks grew a shade more leaden. "T-two months ago!" he stammered painfully; "but that's not p-possible. They—they've given me up. They've f-forgotten me. They th-think I'm dead. After fifteen years? My God, Pete! Why didn't you tell me?" He pleaded the last with a shaken sort of sharpness, in pitiful contrast to the bombast of the preceding speech.

"I didn't see the good of telling you. I was waiting until this trip to see if the picture was still there, and maybe to ask some questions."

"What does it mean?" whispered Bella.

"It means they've some fresh reason to hunt me—some fresh impulse—God knows what or why. How can we tell out here, buried in the snows of fifteen winters. Well!" He struck his hands down on the table edge and stood up. He drew his mouth into a crooked smile and looked at the other two as a naughty child looks at its doting but disapproving elders. The smile transfigured his ugliness. "I've a fancy to see that picture. Want to be reminded of what I looked like fifteen years ago. I was a handsome fellow then. I'm going to take the pelts."

Pete looked dumbly up at him, his lips parted. Bella twisted her apron about her hands. Both seemed to know the hopelessness of protest. In the same anxious dumbness they watched Garth make ready for his trip. As he pulled his cap down close about his ears, Pete at last found his voice.

"Hugh," he began doubtfully, "I wish you wouldn't risk it. We can get on without supplies until next trading-day, when I'll surely be all right."

"Hold your tongue! I'm going," was the answer. "I tell you, the spirit of adventure has me. Who knows what I may meet with out there?" He flung back the door and, pointing with a long arm, stood silhouetted against the dazzle.

"Beauty? Opportunity? Danger? Hope? Death? I shan't shirk it this time. I'll meet whatever comes. But—" He came back a step into the room. His harsh face melted to a shamefaced gentleness; his voice softened. "If they get me down there, if I *don't* come back, you two try to think kindly of me, will you? I know what you think of me now. I know you won't see me as I am—no one but God will ever do me that kindness; but you two—be easy with me in your memories."

Bella, her arms now twisted to their red elbows in her apron, took a few stiff steps across the floor. Her face was expressionless, her eyes lowered. Garth smiled at them both and went out, shutting the door. They heard him singing as he put on his skis:

> *A hundred men were riding,*
>
> *A-hunting for Pierre.*
>
> *They rode and rode, but nothing could they find.*
>
> *They rode around by moonlight;*
>
> *They rode around by day;*
>
> *They rode and rode, but nothing could they find.*

Then came the sharp scraping of his runners across the surface of the snow on a level with the buried roof. It lessened from a hissing speech to a hissing whisper. It sighed away. Bella sat down abruptly on a chair, pulled in her chin like an unhappy child; her bosom lifted as though a sob would force its way out.

"If he doesn't come back!" she murmured. "If he doesn't come back!" She was speaking to God.

CHAPTER II

Pete blinked, swallowed hard and began to talk fast and hopefully.

"He'll come back. I don't believe he'll get halfway there, Bella," he reassured the woman. "He'll come to his senses. You know how moody he is. Come over here and doctor up my ankle, please. 'Make a fuss over me, Bell.' Isn't that what I used to say?"

He coaxed until at last she came and knelt before him and removed his moccasin and heavy woolen sock. The strong white foot was like marble, but the ankle was swollen and discolored. Bella clicked her tongue. "He *is* a brute, you know!" She laughed shortly. Since Garth's departure she had become almost a human being. The deaf-mute look had melted from her, and a sardonic humor emerged; her eyes cleared; she could even smile. "Why do we care so much for him, Pete—the two of us?"

Pete winced under her touch and puckered his brows. "Because he's such a kid, I guess. He's always fretting after the moon."

"Don't you ever get angry with him, Pete? He does treat you shameful sometimes."

"N-no. Not often. He's always sorry and ashamed afterward. He'd like to be as kind as God. I believe if he could only fool us into thinking he *was* God, he could act like Him—ouch, Bella! Go easy."

"You're an awful smart boy, Pete. It's a sin you've never had any schooling."

"Schooling! Gosh! I've had all the schooling I could digest. Hugh beat it into me. He's taught me all he had in his head and a whole lot he never ought to have had there, I guess. But *you've* taught me most, Bella—that's the truth of it."

"*Me!* I never knew anything. They saw to that. They never did anything for me at home but abuse me. Hugh Garth was the only relation I ever had in the world that spoke kind to me. Remember how I used to run over from my folks to tuck you into bed in your little room above the shop, Pete? No, you were too little."

"Of course, I remember," the boy replied. "The ankle's fine now, Bella. Let up. I can't stand that rubbing. Let me stick the foot up on another chair. There—that's great. It doesn't hurt near so bad now. I remember Hugh's bookshop; yes, I do—honest! I remember sitting on the ladder and listening to him talk to the students when they came in. He always was a gorgeous talker, Bella. They used to stand around and listen to his yarns like kids to a fairy story. Just the same as you and I do now—when we can get him into a good humor. But, you know, he used to like strangers best—to talk to, I mean."

Bella assented, bitterly. She had begun to clear the table of its almost untouched meal. "Because he could put it over better with a stranger. It isn't the *truth* Hugh likes—about himself, or others."

Pete had begun to whittle a piece of wood. He was a charming figure, slouching down in his chair, slim and graceful, his shapely golden head ruffled, his chin pressed against his chest. His expression was indescribably sweet and boyish, the shadow of anxiety and pain accentuating a wistful if determined cheerfulness. He was deliberately entertaining Bella, diverting her mind from its agony of apprehension. She saw through him, but like a sick child she took the entertainment languidly.

"Now, *you're* too dead bent on the truth, Bella. You know you are. You're a regular bear for the truth."

"I can't see anything else," she said gloomily. "Things are just so to me—no blinking them."

He put his head a little to one side and contemplated her. "What do you see when you look into the water-bucket, Bella?"

"The water-bucket?" She flushed. "Just because you caught me prinking that once!"

"Well, if you had a mirror, what would you see in it, then?"

"An ugly old woman, Pete."

"There! Your mind's just the wrong-side-out of Hugh's. He won't see himself ugly, and you won't see yourself pretty. I'm the only sane fellow in this house."

"And you never in your life saw a pretty woman to remember her. Besides, you're too young." She said it with a tart sweetness and vanished into the kitchen.

With her departure Pete's whittling ceased, his hands fell slack and he began to stare out through the snow-walled window. His anxiety for Hugh slipped imperceptibly into a vague pondering over his own youthfulness. That's what those two were always telling him, sometimes savagely, sometimes tenderly! "You're too young." What did it mean to him, anyhow, that he was "too young"? A desolation from which at times he suffered in secret overcame him.

He was twenty-one or -two—or his memory lied. They had never celebrated his birthdays, but he was five or six years old when Hugh had been so suddenly, so unexplainably taken from the house, back there in the little Eastern college town where they had lived. It was a few months later that Bella—Cousin Bella, who worked at "the farm"—came for him, a furtive, desperate Bella with a bruised face—a Bella tight-strung for flight, for a breaking of the galling accustomed ties of her life, for a terrible plunge into unknown adventure. She had muttered to him, as she dressed him and bundled together a few of his belongings, that they "were going to Hugh"—only it was another name she used, a name since blotted from their lives.

Hugh had sent for them. She was the only person in the world that Hugh could trust. But no one must know where they were going. They must be away by the time the man who took charge of the shop came back in the morning.

Pete remembered the journey. He remembered the small frontier station where they left the train at last. He remembered that strange, far-flung horizon, streaked with dawn, and his first taste of the tangy, heady air. There had been a long, long drive and a parting with the friendly driver where Bella turned on to the trail through the woods. It had been dim and dark and terrible among the endless regiments of trees—mazy and green and altogether bewildering. And after vague hop-o'-my-thumb wanderings, he had a disconnected memory of Hugh—a wild, rugged, ragged, bearded Hugh who caught him up fiercely as though he had an ogrish hunger for the feel of little boys. It was night when they came to Hugh's hiding-place. For miles Pete had been carried in his brother's arms. Bella had limped behind them. There had been a ford, he remembered; the splashing water had roused Pete, and he stayed awake afterward until he found himself before a dancing fire of logs in a queer, dark, resinous-smelling house, very low, with unglazed windows. He remembered, too, that Bella had burst out crying. That was the queerest memory of them all—that crying of Bella's.— Even now he could not understand exactly why she had cried so then.

The frightened, furtive life they had all led since—the life of scared wild things—had left its mark on Pete. His fear for Hugh now threw him back into the half-forgotten state of apprehension which had been the atmosphere of all his little boyhood. He had not known then why strange men were creatures to be feared and shunned. In fact, he had never been told the reason for Hugh's flight. Only, bit by bit, he had pieced together hints and vague allusions until he knew that this strange, embittered, boasting poet of a brother had killed or had been accused of killing. In his loyal boy mind Hugh Garth was promptly acquitted. It was the world that was wrong—not Hugh. Yet to-day, after all the long years of carefulness, he had gone back to the cruelty of the world.

Like a beast the boy's anxiety for his brother began to prowl about the walls of his mind. He imagined Hugh appearing at the trading-station. He pictured the curious glances of the Indians and the white natives. This limping, extravagant, energetic Hugh with his whitening hair and eyebrows and flaring hazel eyes—with his crooked nose and mouth, his magnificently desperate manner and his magnificently desperate voice—attention would inevitably fasten upon him anywhere; how much more in an empty land such as this! Pete fancied the inquiring looks turned from the man to the man's posted picture. It was no longer a faithful likeness, of course; still, it was a likeness. There was no other man in all the world like Hugh! He was made of odd, fantastic fragments, of ill-fitting parts—physically, mentally, spiritually. It was as if a soul had seen itself in a crooked mirror and had fashioned a form to match the distorted image. Hugh wouldn't, couldn't force himself to be inconspicuous. He would swagger; he would talk loud; his big, beautiful voice would challenge attention, create an audience. He would have some impossible, splendid tale to tell.

Pete sat up straighter in his chair, gingerly rearranging the ankle, and lifted his blue and haunted eyes—the eyes of the North—to the window.

The dazzle of noon had faded to a glow. The short winter day was nearly done. There would be a long violet twilight, and then, the blaze of stars.

But for his aching ankle Pete would be sliding out on soundless skis, now poised for breathless flight down some long slope, now leaping fallen trees or buried ditches. He spent half of his wild young restlessness in such long night runs when, in a sort of ecstasy, he outraced the stifled longings of his exiled youth. But there would be no ski-running for several nights now. He was a prisoner, and at a time when imprisonment was hard to bear.

If only there were some way of getting quick news of Hugh! Why had Bella and he let this thing happen? Why had they stood helplessly by and allowed the rash fool to go singing to his own destruction? They might have held him by force, if not by argument, long enough to bring him to his senses. They had been weak; they were always weak before Hugh's magnetic strength—always the audience, the following; Bella, for all her devastating tongue, no less than himself. And Hugh's liberty, perhaps his life, might be the price of their acquiescence.

Straining forward in his chair, listening, there came to Pete, across the silence, the sound of skis.

He rose and hopped to the door, flinging it wide. He could not see above the top of the drift which rose just beyond the roof to a height of nine or ten feet, but listening intently, he thought he recognized a familiar slight unevenness in the sliding of the skis.

"Bella!" he shouted, his boy-voice ringing with relief. "Bella! Here's Hugh. He's come back."

Bella was instantly at his side. They stood waiting in the doorway. Against the violet sky darkening above the blue wall of snow, a bulky figure rose, blotting out the light. It half slid, half tumbled down upon them, clumsy and shapeless.

"Let us in," panted Hugh. "Let us in."

Slipping his feet from the straps of his skis, he staggered past them and they saw that he was carrying a woman in his arms.

CHAPTER III

"Shut the door," Hugh whispered, and laid his burden down on a big black bear-hide near the stove. He knelt beside it. He had no eyes for anything else. Pete, hobbling to him, gazed curiously down, and Bella knelt opposite and drew away Hugh's mackinaw coat, with which he had wrapped his trove. It was not a woman whom they looked down upon, but a girl, and very young—perhaps not yet seventeen—a girl with cropped dark curly hair and a face so wan and blue and at the same time so scorched by the snow-glare that its exquisiteness of feature was all the more marked. Hugh's handkerchief was tied loosely across her eyes.

"I heard her crying in the snow," he said with ineffable tenderness; "crying like a little bleating lamb with cold and pain and hunger and fright—the most pitiful thing in God's cruel trap of life. She's blind—snow-blind."

Pete gave a sharp exclamation, and Bella gently removed the handkerchief. The small figure moaned and moved its head. The lids of her eyes were swollen and discolored.

"Snow-blind," echoed Bella.

"A bad case," said Hugh. "Get her some soup, Bella, and—perhaps, hot water—I don't know." He looked up helplessly.

Bella went to the kitchen. She had regained her old look of dumbness. Beside the figure on the floor Pete touched one of the girl's small clenched hands. It was like ice. At the touch she moaned, and Hugh ordered sharply: "Let her alone." So the boy dragged himself up again and stood by the mantel, watching Hugh with puzzled and wondering eyes.

"Think what she's been through," Hugh murmured, "that little delicate thing, wandering for two days, out in this cold—scared by the woods, blinded by the pain, starving. When I found her, you'd have thought she'd be afraid of a wild man like me, but she just lifted up her arms like a baby and dropped her head on my shoulder. She—she patted my cheek—"

Bella brought the soup, and Hugh, raising the small black head on the crook of his arm, forced a spoonful between the clenched teeth. The girl swallowed and began again to whimper: "Oh, my eyes! My eyes! They hurt me so!" She turned her face against Hugh's chest and clung to him.

"They'll be better soon," he soothed her; then fiercely to Bella: "Can't we do something? Don't you know what to do?"

Again Bella went to the kitchen, moving like an automaton. Hugh coaxed and murmured, feeding the girl in spite of her pain. He managed to force a little of the soup down her throat, and a faint stain of color came back to her lips and cheeks. Bella presently reappeared with salve and lotion, and Hugh helped her hold the swollen lids apart, his big hands very skillful, while she gently washed out the eyes. Then they put the salve on her sun-scorched face. She sighed as though in some relief, and again snuggled against Hugh.

"Don't go away, please," she pleaded in a sweet trickle of voice. "I'm scared to feel you gone. You're so warm. You're so strong. Will you talk to me again, please? Your voice is so comforting, so beau-ti-ful."

So Hugh talked. The others drew away and watched and listened. They did not look at each other. For some reason Pete was ashamed to meet Bella's eyes. As usual, they were the audience, those two. They sat, each in a chair, the width of the room apart; below them, his grizzled head and warped face transfigured by its new tenderness, Hugh bent over the child in his arms. Pete held his tumult of curiosity, of interest, in leash. He could hear his heart pounding.

"You're safe now, and warm," Hugh was murmuring. "No need to be scared, no need. I'll take care of you. Go to sleep. I'm strong enough to keep off anything. You're safe and snug as a little bird in its nest. That's right. Go to sleep."

Pete's blue eyes dwelt on this amazing spectacle with curious wonder. This was a Hugh he had never seen before. For the first time in fifteen years, he realized, the man had forgotten himself.

CHAPTER IV

To Hugh Garth the girl told her story at last. She seemed to realize only dimly that there were two other living beings in this house, to her a house of darkness peopled only by voices—Pete's modest, rare boy speeches, Bella's brief, smothered statements. The great music of Hugh's utterance must indeed have filled her narrowed world. So it was to him she turned— he was always near her, sitting on the pelt beside the chair to which, after a day and night in Bella's bed, she was helped.

She had a charming fashion of speech, rather slow motions of her lips, which had some difficulty with "r" and "s," a difficulty which she evidently struggled against conscientiously, and as she talked, she gesticulated with her slim little hands. She was a touching thing sitting there in Hugh's carved throne—he an abdicated monarch at her feet, knee in hand, grizzled head tilted back, hazel eyes raised to her and filled with adoration.

"I am called Sylvie Doone," she said with that quaint struggle over the "S." "I was always miserable at home." She gave the quick sigh of a child. "You see, my father died when I was very little, and then my mother married again. We lived in the grimmest little town, hardly more than a dozen houses, beside a stream, up in Massachusetts—farming country, but poor farming, hard farming, the kind that twists the men with rheumatism, and makes the women all pinched and worn. Mother was like that. She died when I was thirteen. You see—there I was, so queerly fixed. I had to live with Mr. Pynche—there was no other home for me anywhere. And he kind of resented it. He had enough money not to need me for work—a sister of his did the housework better than I could—and yet he was poor enough to hate having to feed me and pay for my clothes. I was always feeling in the way, and a burden. There was nothing I could do.

"Then I saw something about the movies in a magazine, and pictures of girls, not much better-looking than me, making lots of money. I borrowed some money from a drug-store clerk who wanted to keep company with me—I've paid it back—and I went to New York. I did get a job. But I'm not a good actress."

She faltered over the rest—a commonplace story of engagements, of failures, until she found herself touring the West with a wretched theatrical troupe. "We were booked for a little town off there beyond your woods, and the train was stalled in a snowstorm. We got on a stage-coach, but it got stuck in a drift on one of those dreadful roads. I was freezing cold, and I thought I'd make a short cut through the woods. The road was running along the edge of a big forest of pines. I cut off while they were all working to dig out the horses.

"Mr. Snaring said, 'Look out for the bears!' and I laughed and ran up what looked like a snow-buried trail. There was a hard crust. The woods were all glittering and so beautiful. I ran into them, laughing. I was so glad to get away by myself from those people into the woods where it was so silent and sort of solemn—like being in a church again. I can't think how I got so lost. I meant to come round back to the road, but before I knew it, I didn't know which way the road was. The pines were so dense, so all alike, they looked almost as if they kept sort of shifting about me. I tried to follow back on my footprints, but in some places snow had shaken down from the branches. And there were so many—so dreadfully many other tracks—of animals—" She put her hands over her face and shrank down in her chair.

"Forget about them, Sylvie," Hugh admonished gently. "Even if there had been bears about, they wouldn't likely have bothered you any."

"I can't bring myself to tell you about that time—I can't!"

"Don't, then—only, how did you live through the night, my dear?"

"I don't know—except that I never stayed still. I got out from the trees because I was afraid of bears, and I lost my hat. The sun was like fire shining up from underneath and down from up above. My eyes began to hurt almost at once, and by the time night came, it was agony. The darkness didn't seem to help me any either; the glare still seemed to come in under my lids. I couldn't sleep for the pain. I knew I'd freeze if I stood still, so I kept moving all night, trampling round in circles, I suppose. Next morning the terrible glare began again. Then everything went red. I was nearly crazy when you found me, Mr. Garth."

"Please call me Hugh," he murmured, taking her hand in his. "I feel in a way that you belong to me now—I saved you from dying alone there in the cold and brought you back to my home. I've got jettison rights, Sylvie." She let him hold her hand, and flushed.

"You'll never know what it felt like to hear your voice call to me, to feel you pulling me up. I'd only just dropped a few minutes before, but I'd never have struggled up. It would have been the end." She trembled in the memory, and he patted her hand. "I don't know why a man like you lives off here in this wild place, but thank God, you do live here! Though," she added with wistfulness, twisting her soft mouth, "though I can't ever quite see why God should care much for a Sylvie Doone." She touched the lids of her closed eyes. "I wonder why it doesn't worry me more not to be able to see. Now that the pain's gone, I don't seem to care much."

"Thank God. Perhaps, though," he added half-grudgingly, "in a few days you'll see again."

She smiled. "I'd just love to see *you*. You must be wonderful!"

"What makes you think that?" he asked, his warped face glowing.

"You're so strong and young, such thick hair, such finely shaped hands and such a voice." Sylvie's associates had been of a profession that deals perpetually in personalities. "If I'd been blind a long time, I suppose I could just run my hand over your face, and I'd know what you look like. But I can't tell a thing." She felt for his face and brushed it eagerly with her fingers, laughing at herself. "I just know that you have thick eyelashes and are clean-shaven. Is Bella your wife? And that big little boy your son?"

He started. "No, she's a faithful thing, the boy's nurse. And the kid's my young brother—a great gawk of a boy for his age, a regular bean-pole."

"It's so hard to tell anything about people if you can't see them. I wouldn't have thought he was so big. Is he about fourteen or fifteen? He speaks so low and gently; he might be any age."

"And a man's height—pretty near too big to lick, though he needs it."

"And Bella, what's she like?"

"A dried-up mummy of a woman."

The kitchen door creaked. Hugh started and shot a look over his shoulder. Bella stood on the kitchen threshold with an expressionless face and lowered eyelids.

"Why did you jump?" asked Sylvie nervously.

Hugh wet his lips with his tongue. "Nothing. The door creaked. Go on. Tell me more, child," he urged.

"No. I want to hear about you now. Tell me your story."

Hugh clenched his hands and flushed darkly. He glanced over his shoulder with a furtive look, but Bella had gone.

"No one else rightly knows my story, Sylvie. Will you promise me never to speak of it, to Bella, to Pete, to any one?"

"Of course, I promise." Her face beamed with the pride of a child entrusted with a secret.

Then, lowering his voice and moving closer to her chair, he began a fictitious history, a history of persecuted and heroic innocence, of reckless adventure, of daring self-sacrifice. The girl listened with parted lips. Her cheeks glowed. And behind the door, Bella too listened, straining her ears.

The murmur of Hugh's recital, rising now and then to some melodramatic climax, then dropping cautiously, rippled on, broken now and again by Sylvie's ejaculations. Behind the door Bella stood like a wooden block, colorless and stolid as though she understood not a syllable of what she heard. But after a rigid hour she faltered away, stumbled across the kitchen and out into the snow.

There, in the broad light of the setting sun, Pete rhythmically bent and straightened over his saw. The tool sang with a hissing, ringing rhythm, and the young man drove it with a lithe, long swing of body, forward and back, forward and back, in alternate postures of untiring grace. The air was not cold. There was the cloudy softness premonitory of a spring storm; the sun glowed like a dying fire through a long, narrow rift in the shrouded west. Pete had thrown aside his coat and drawn in his belt. The collar of his flannel shirt was open and turned back; his head was bare. The bright gold of his short hair, the scarlet of his cheeks, the vivid blue of his brooding eyes, made shocks of color against the prevailing whiteness. Even the indigo of his overalls and the dark gray of his shirt stood out with a curious value of tint and texture. His bare hands and forearms glowed. He was whistling with a boy's vigor and a bird's sweetness.

Bella caught Pete's arm as it bent for one of the strong forward sweeps. He stopped, let go of his saw, and turned to her, smiling.

Then—the smile gone: "What's wrong?"

Her eyes flamed in her pale, tense face. "We've got to stop it, Pete," she said. "It's horrible!"

"What? Don't stand out here with those bare arms, Bella." He was pulling his own shirt-sleeves down over his glistening bronze forearms as he spoke.

"We can't talk in the house," she said, "and I've got to talk. I—Do you know what Hugh's doing—what he's telling that girl? What he's letting her believe?"

Pete shook his head, but at the same time turned his blue eyes away from her toward the glowing west.

"Lies," said Bella. She laughed a short, explosive laugh. "He's got his ideal audience at last—a blind one. She thinks he's young and handsome and heroic. Pete, she thinks he's a hero. She thinks he's buried himself out here for the sake of somebody else. Oh, it's a regular romance, and it's been going on for hours—it's still going on. By now he believes it all himself.

He's putting in the details. And Sylvie: 'Oh!' she's saying, and 'Ah, Mr. Garth, how you must have suffered! How wonderful you are!' And—look at me Pete—do you want to know what we are—according to him—you and I?"

He did not turn his eyes from the west, even when she shook his arm.

"I'm a dried-up mummy of a woman—faithful?—yes, I'm faithful—an old servant. And you're a child, an overgrown bean-pole of a boy, fourteen or fifteen years old."

The young man stood tall and still—a statue of golden youth in the golden light—the woman clutching at his arm, her face twisted, her eyes afire, all the colorlessness of her body and the suppressed flame of her spirit pitilessly apparent.

"Look at me, Pete."

"Well," he sighed gently, "what of it?" He looked down at her and smiled. "It's the first good time he's had for fifteen years. You know we don't make him happy. I don't grudge him his joy, Bella, do you? It can't last long, anyway. Fairy tales can't hurt her—Hugh believes—almost—in his own inventions. She'll be going back—her friends will be hunting for her. I'll let her think I'm a bean-pole of a boy if it makes him any happier to have me one. And why do you care?"

She drew in her breath. "Oh, I don't suppose I care—so much," she said haltingly. "But—think of the girl."

His eyes widened a little and fell. "The girl?"

"She's falling in love with him!"

Pete threw back his head and laughed aloud. "Oh, Bella, you know, *that's* funny!"

"It's not. It's tragic. It's horrible. You'll see. Watch her face."

"I have watched it." He spoke dreamily. "It's a very pretty and sweet face."

"Pete, Hugh's robbing *you.*"

"Me?"

"Yes, you're young. You're ready for loving. This child—God sent her to you, to get you out of this desolation, to lead you back to loving and living, to give you what you ought to have—Life."

It was as though she had struck him. He started and drew himself away. "Shut up, Bella," he said with boyish roughness and limped past her into the house.

CHAPTER V

In these days Hugh must have known that his magic-making, as he led the little blind girl through the forest of his romancing, was at the mercy of those two that knew him for what he really was; except for queer, wild, threatening looks now and again, he gave no sign. He played his part magnificently, even trusting them to come in with help when they were given their cue. He had dominated them for so long that even they and the picture of him that they held in their minds were not so real as his dreams. It was a queer game, queer and breathless, played in this narrow space shut in by the white wilderness. And as the slow days went by, the low log house seemed to be filled more and more with smothered and conflicting emotions. A dozen times the whole extravaganza came near collapse; a dozen times Hugh saved it by a word, or Pete and Bella by a silence. Their parts were not easy, and although Pete still smiled, his young clear face grew whiter and more strained. Sylvie treated him always as though he were a child. She would pat his head and rumple his hair if he sat near her; once, suddenly, she kissed him lightly on the cheek, after he had moved the chair for her.

"You're a dear, quiet boy," she said. "I frightened you to death, then, didn't I? Hasn't anyone ever kissed you before?" His cheek burned so that, touching it with her fingers, she laughed. "I've made you blush, poor kid! I know. Boys hate petting, don't they? You'll have to get used to it, Pete, because I mean to pet you—oh, a lot! You need some one to draw you out. These two people snub you too much. Boys of fourteen aren't quite children, after all, are they? Besides, they're interesting. I know. I was fourteen myself not such ages back. You're not cross, are you, Pete?"

His eyes were misty, and his hands were cold. He could not understand his own emotion, his own pain. He muttered something and got himself away. She called him "sullen" and was angry with him, complaining to Hugh at supper that "Petey" had been "a bear" to her. Hugh simulated a playful annoyance and began to scold; then a sort of nervous fury came over him. He stamped and struck the table and snarled at Pete. The young man rose at his place and stared at his brother silently. There were two splotches of deep color on his cheeks. Sylvie protested: "Don't, please, be so angry with him. I was only teasing, just in fun. Bella, tell Hugh to stop. I had no business to kiss Pete. But I just wanted to pet something."

Hugh's threatening suddenly stopped, and Pete sat down. In the strained silence Bella laughed. Her laughter had the sound of a snapped bow-string. Sylvie had pushed her chair back a little from the table and was turning her head quickly from one to the other of them. Her mouth showed a tremble of uncertainty. It was easy to see that she sensed a tension, a confusion. Hugh leaned forward and broke into a good-humored rattle of speech, and as Pete and Bella sat silent, Sylvie gradually was reassured. Near the end of the meal she put out her hand toward Pete.

"Please don't be so cross with me, Pete! Give me a shake for forgiveness."

He touched her hand, his eyes lowered, and drew his fingers away. She laughed.

"How shy you are—a wild, forest thing! I'll have to civilize you."

"Leave him alone," admonished Hugh softly, "leave him alone."

As he said this, he did not look at Sylvie, but gazed somberly at Pete. It was a strange look, at once appealing and threatening, pitiful and dangerous. Pete fingered his fork nervously. Finally Bella stood up and began to clear the table with an unaccustomed clatter of noisy energy.

"How long are you going to keep it up, Pete?" she asked him afterward. He was helping her wash the dishes, drying them deftly with a piece of flour-sacking.

"Since we've let it begin, we'll have to go on with it to a finish," he answered coldly. "After all"—he paused, polished a platter and turned away to put it on its shelf—"he's not doing anything so dreadful—just twisting the facts a little. I *am* an ignorant lout. I might as well be fourteen, for all I know."

"And I *am* a mummy of a woman?"

In pity for her he made to put his arm about her. "Don't be a goose, Bella," he said, but she flung his hand from her. "Why does it make you so sore and angry?" he asked wistfully. "Hugh is not pretty to look at, but perhaps Sylvie sees him better than we do—in a way; and if she learns to love him while she's blind, then, when she sees him, if she ever sees him—"

"Chances are she never will. If her eyes don't get better soon, they likely never will."

"Isn't it horrible?"

"You don't seem to think so. So long's she has Hugh to paint pictures for her, what does she need eyes for? What's to come of it, Pete? She's falling in love with the fine figure of a hero he's made her believe he is. But how can he marry her?"

"Couldn't he go off somewhere else and marry her and start again? Honest, I think if Hugh had some one who thought he was a god, he'd likely enough be one. He—he lives by—illusion—isn't that the word? It's kind of easy to be noble when some one you love believes you to be, isn't it? That's Hugh; he—"

Bella threw down her rag, turned fiercely upon him and gripped his shoulders.

"Are you a man or a child?" she said. "You love this girl yourself!"

"No!" he cried and broke from her and went limping out into the frosty night with its comfortless glitter of stars.

As soon as his ankle was stronger, Pete spent all day and most of the night on his skis, trying to outrun the growing shadow of his misery. Hugh's work fell on his shoulders. He had not only his accustomed chores, the Caliban duties of woodchopping and water-carrying, the dressing of wild meat, the dish-drying and heavier housework, the repairs about the cabin—but he had the trapping. In Hugh's profound new absorption he seemed to have forgotten the necessity for making a livelihood. During the first years of their exile they had lived on his savings, ordering their supplies by the mail, which left them at the foot of that distant trail leading into the forest. Thence Hugh, under shelter of night, would carry them—lonely, terrible journeys that taxed even his strength. When Pete grew big enough to load, he was sent to the trading-station, and Hugh became an expert trapper. The savings were not entirely spent, but they were no longer touched; the pelts brought a livelihood.

Pete had had his instructions concerning his behavior at the trading-station; many years before, he had stammered a legend of a sickly father who had died, who was buried back there by the lonely cabin where he and his "mother" chose to live. Bella and Hugh had even dug up a mound for which they had fashioned a rude cross. It could be seen, in summer, from the living-room window—that mock grave more terrible in its suggestions than a real grave ever could have been. There was also a hiding-place under the boards of the floor. No one had ever seen the grave or driven Hugh into hiding. It was not an inquisitive country, and its desolation was forbidding. Pete had learned to discourage the rare sociability of the other traders.

Now, however, the young man had not only to trade his pelts but to trap them, and for this business of trapping which was distasteful to him, he had not a tithe of Hugh's skill. His bundle of pelts brought him a sorry supply of necessities. He was ashamed, himself, and having dumped the burden from his shoulders to the kitchen floor would hurry into the other room, not to see Bella's expression when she opened her bundles.

To-night Pete was tired; the load had not been heavy, but the snow was beginning to soften under the mild glowing of an April sun, and his skis had tugged at his feet and gathered a clogging mass. His body ached, and there was a sullen and despairing weight upon his spirit. A mob of rebels danced in his heart. He watched Hugh's face, saw the flaring adoration of his eyes, thought that Sylvie must feel the scorch of them on her cheek, so close. In his own eyes there showed a brooding fire.

Bella broke into the room.

"Look here," she said, "you'd better get to trapping again, Hugh Garth. Pete's pelts don't bring a quarter of what we need—especially these days."

Sylvie quivered as though a wound had been touched. "Oh, you mean me," she said, "I know you mean me. I'm making trouble. I'm eating too much. I'll go. Pete, has anybody been asking about me at the post-office, trying to find me? They *must* be hunting for me." She had stood up and was clasping and unclasping her hands. Hugh and Pete protested in one breath: "Nonsense, Sylvie!"

And Pete went on with: "There hasn't been anyone asking about you, but—so much the better for us. You're safe here, and comfortable, aren't you? And—Hugh, *you* tell her what it means to us to have her here."

It was more of a speech than he had made since Sylvie's arrival, and it was not just the speech, in tone or manner, of a fourteen-year-old boy. There was a new somber note in his voice, too—some of the youthful quality had gone out of it. Sylvie took a step toward him, to thank him, perhaps, perhaps to satisfy, by laying her hand upon him, a sudden bewilderment; but in her blindness she stumbled on the edge of the hearth, and to save her from falling, Pete caught her in his arms. For an instant he held her close, held her fiercely, closer and more fiercely than he knew, and Sylvie felt the strength of him and heard the pounding of his heart. Then Hugh plucked her away with a smothered oath. He put her into a chair, crushed her hand in one of his, and turned upon Bella.

"Go back into the kitchen," he ordered brutally; "trapping's not your business. You mind your cooking."

"Be careful, Hugh!" Bella's whisper whistled like a falling lash, "I'll not stand that tone from you. Be careful!"

"Oh," pleaded Sylvie, "why do you all quarrel so? Off here by yourselves with nobody else to care, I'd think you would just love each other. I love you all—yes, I do, even you, Bella, though I know you hate *me*. Bella, *why* do you hate me? Why does it make you so angry to have me here? Does it make your work so much harder? I'll soon be better; I'm learning to feel my way about. I'll be able to help you. I should think you'd be glad to have a girl in the house—another woman. I'm sorry to be a nuisance, really I am. I'd go if I could."

The lonely, deep silence, always waiting to fall upon them, shut down with suddenness at the end of her sweet, tearful quaver of appeal. For minutes no one spoke. Then Pete followed Bella out of the room. She had not answered Sylvie's beseeching questions, but had only stood with lowered head, her face working, her hands twisting her dress. She had run out just as her face cramped as though for tears.

When the other two had gone, Hugh captured both of Sylvie's hands in his. "You don't mean that, do you?" he asked brokenly. "You don't mean you'd go away if you could, Sylvie!"

At Hugh's voice she started and the color rushed into her cheeks. "If I make you quarrel, if I'm a nuisance, if Pete and Bella hate me so!"

"But I"—he said—"I love you." He drew her head—she was sitting in her chair again—against his side. "No, don't smile at me like that; I don't mean the sort of love you think. I love you terribly. Can't you feel how I love you? Listen, close against my heart. Don't be frightened. There, now you know how I love you!"

He rained kisses on her head resting droopingly against him.

"How can a man like you love *me*?" she asked with wistful uncertainty.

"A man like me?" Hugh groaned. "Ah, but I do—I do! You must stay with me always. Sylvie, somehow we will be married—you—and I!"

"Now it frightens me," she whispered, "being blind. It does frighten me now. I want so terribly to see your face, your eyes. Oh, you mustn't marry a blind girl, a waif. You've been so noble, you've suffered so terribly. You ought to have some wonderful woman who would understand your greatness, would see all that you are."

"Now," he sighed, "now I *am* great—because you think I am; that's water to me—after a lifetime of thirst."

"Hugh, *am* I good enough for you?" She was sobbing and laughing at the same time.

It was too much for him. He drew himself gently away. He whispered: "I can't bear being loved—being happy. I'll go out by myself for a bit alone. Sylvie, Sylvie! Every instant I—I worship *you*!" He threw himself down before her and pressed his face against her knees. She caressed the thick, grizzled hair. He stood up and then stumbled away from her, more blind than she, out of the house into the gathering night.

CHAPTER VI

In the big, rudely carved chair Sylvie leaned back her head and pressed her hands to her unseeing eyes. She was not sorry that Hugh had left her, for she was oppressed and unnerved by her own emotions. Until he had kissed her hair, she had not known that she loved him—or rather loved an invisible presence that had enveloped her in an atmosphere of sympathy, of protection, that had painted itself, so to speak, in heroic colors and proportions against her darkness, that had revealed both strength and tenderness in touch and movement, and warm, deep voice.

For until now Sylvie's life had been entirely lacking in protection and tenderness; she had never known sympathy—her natural romanticism had been starved. The lacks in her life Hugh had supplied the more lavishly because he was aided, in her blindness, by the unrestricted powers of her fancy. But now in all the fervor of this, Sylvie felt, also for the first time, the full bitterness of her blindness. If she could see him—if only once! If she could see him!

And there came to Sylvie unreasonably, disconnectedly, a keen memory of Pete's embrace when he had caught her up from falling on the hearth. A boy of fourteen? Strange that he should be so strong, that his heart should beat so loud, that his arms should draw themselves so closely, so powerfully about her. What were they really like, these people who moved unseen around her and who exerted such great power over her sudden helplessness?

She got up and began to walk to and fro restlessly, gropingly across the room. She wished now that Hugh would come back. He had been with her so constantly that she had grown utterly dependent upon him. The dense red fog that lay so thick about her, frightened her when Hugh was not there to keep her mind busy with his talk to paint pictures for her, to command her with his magnetic presence. She stood still and strained her eyes. She *must* see again. If she tried hard, the red fog would surely lift. Happiness, and her new love, they would be strong enough to dispel the mist. There— already it was a shade lighter! She almost thought that she could make out the brightness of the fire. She went toward it and sat down on the bear-skin, holding out her tremulous, excited hands. And with a sudden impulse toward confidence she called: "Pete, O Pete! Come here a moment, please."

He came, and she beckoned to him with a gesture and an upward, vaguely directed smile, to sit beside her. She was aware of the rigid reserve of his body holding itself at a distance.

"Pete," she said wistfully, "what can I do to make you love me?"

He uttered a queer, sharp sound, but said nothing.

"Are you jealous?"

"No, Sylvie," he muttered.

"Oh, how I wish I could see you, Pete! I know then I'd understand you better. Pete, try to be a little more—more human. Tell me about yourself. Haven't you a bit of fondness for me? You see, I want—Pete—some day perhaps I'll be your sister—"

"Then he has asked you to marry him?"

He was usually so quiet that she was startled at this new tone.

"Don't," she said. "Hush! We have only just found out. He went away because he couldn't bear his own happiness. Pete—" She felt for him and her hand touched his cheek. "Oh, Pete, your face is wet. You're crying."

"No, I'm not," he denied evenly. "It was melting from the roof when I came in."

She sighed. "You are so strange, Pete. Will you let me kiss you now— since you are going to be my big little brother?"

"I can't," he whispered. "I can't."

She laughed and crooked her arm about his neck, forcing his face down to hers. His lips were hard and cool.

The face that Sylvie imagined a boy's face, shy and blushing, half frightened, half cross, perhaps a trifle pleased, was so white and patient a face in its misery that her blind tenderness seemed almost like an intentional cruelty. It was an intensity of feeling almost palpable, but Sylvie's mouth remained unburnt, though it removed itself with a pathetic little twist of disappointment.

"You don't need to say anything," she said, "You've shown me how you feel. You can't like me. You are sorry I came. And I want so dreadfully for some one just now to talk to—to help me, to understand. It's all dark and wonderful and frightening. I wish I had a brother—"

She bent her face to her knees and began to cry simply and passionately. At that Pete found it easy to forget himself. He put his arm very carefully about her, laying one of his hands on her bent head and stroking her hair.

"You have a brother," he said. "Right here."

The dark small silken head shook. "No. You don't like me."

"I do—I do. Please tell me everything you feel like telling; I'd like awfully to help you, to understand, to listen to you. You see, you've been so much with Hugh, I haven't had a chance to know you as he does. And I guess—well—maybe I'm sort of shy."

She lifted her head at that, took his stroking hand and held it in both of hers under her chin, as a little girl holds her pet kitten for the pleasure of its warmth. "You must get over being shy with me, Pete. We both love Hugh; we both admire him so. I'd so love to talk to you about him—"

"Then do, Sylvie."

"I've never seen him," she sighed, "and you can see him all day long, Pete; will you try your best now to describe Hugh to me—every bit of him? Tell me the color of his eyes and the shape of his face and—everything. Tell me all you remember about him always."

"I—I'm no good at that, Sylvie. A fellow you see all day long—why, you don't know what he looks like, 'specially if he's your own brother."

"Well, you certainly know the color of his eyes."

"He has hazel eyes—I think you'd call them—"

"Yes?" she drank in his words eagerly, pressing his hand tighter in her excitement. "Go on. If only you were a girl, now, you'd do this so much better."

"I—I—but I don't know what else to say, Sylvie. He is very strong."

"Of course. I know that. Didn't he pick me up out of the snow and carry me home? He moved as though he had a feather on his arm. You are very strong too, Pete—*very* strong. Are *your* eyes hazel?"

"No; blue."

"I always liked blue eyes. I like to imagine that Hugh is just the Viking sort of man I dreamed about when I was a little girl. You think I'm a silly goose, don't you?"

"Yes, rather."

"Don't keep trying to pull your hand away, dear; you can't guess how it comforts me. I'm awfully alone here, and strange. I don't suppose you know how queer and frightening it's been—this getting lost and being brought here in the dark, and then—living on in the dark, just trusting my instincts, my intuitions, instead of my eyes. Voices tell a lot about people, don't they?—more than I ever dreamed they could. Pete, there is nothing in that—that splendid, generous thing Hugh did, the thing I am not to talk about, nothing to keep Hugh now from going back to the world—some place—that is, far away from where it happened—and beginning again, is there?"

"I hope not, Sylvie."

She sighed. "Of course it was wonderful. If he hadn't told me of it, I never should have known half of his greatness; yet I can't help wishing he were free. It's sad to think there will always be the memory of that dreadful suffering and danger in his life."

"Very sad," said Pete.

"How alone we both are—he and I! Bella, and you, Pete—don't be angry, please—I don't think you quite understand Hugh, quite appreciate him."

"Perhaps not."

"He has always been lonely. You are so young, and Bella is so stupid—stupid and cross."

"No, she isn't, Sylvie. I know Bella a lot better than you do. She's not stupid or cross—"

"Well, I like you to stick up for your old nurse. She certainly must have loved you a lot to bring you way out here and to stay here all these years to take care of you. I wonder where she'll go and what she'll do when Hugh and I get married. You're too old for a nurse now, Pete. Do you mind if I lean back against you that way? It's so comfortable. I'd be happier without Bella, Pete, you know."

"Would you, Sylvie? Well, Bella and I will have to go away together somewhere, I guess."

"I didn't say you, dear. I love you a lot—next best to Hugh. There's something awfully sweet about you—you great strong overgrown thing! Your heart goes *thump-thump-thump-thump*, as though it was as big as the sun.... I feel much better and happier now. Things have got steady again. Only—I wish Hugh would come back."

Pete gave a strangled sigh.

"He'll be back." And he began to draw himself away from her. "I think I hear him now, Sylvie."

"Stay where you are," she laughed. "Don't be ashamed of being found with a sister leaning against you and holding your hand. Are you afraid of Hugh? I think sometimes he's rather hard with you—I'll have to speak to him about that. Oh"—in a sudden ecstasy—"how happy I am! I feel as light as the air. I want every one to be happy. Tell me when Hugh comes in how happy he looks, Pete—promise me, quick! There he is at the door now."

"Yes," he whispered, "I promise. Let me go, please, Sylvie."

He pulled himself away and stood up. At the instant, the door was opened and shut quickly, stealthily. It was Hugh, breathing hard, gray with fear.

"They're coming," he said harshly. "Pete, they're after me. Men are coming across the flat."

CHAPTER VII

"Did they see you?" Pete demanded anxiously.

"I don't think so." Hugh was breathing fast; he had evidently fled across the snow at top speed.

"Get in, then, quick—out of sight." Pete was already tearing up boards above that long-waiting place of hiding. Hugh was about to step down into it when he glanced up and saw Sylvie. She was standing as the unseeing stand in moments of frightened bewilderment, her hands clasped, her head turning from side to side. "Look here," whispered Hugh, still absorbed in his own danger, "don't let them know that Sylvie just wandered in here. Don't let them start asking her any questions; it's too dangerous. Let her be—one of the family." He smiled maliciously. "Let her be your wife, Pete." Then, as though that picture had fired his love through its hint of jeopardy, he held out both arms suddenly: "Come here, Sylvie—lead her to me, Pete."

The boy obeyed. But as her uncertain arms trembled about Hugh's shoulders Pete turned sharply away. He heard the quick, anxious murmur of their voices:

"Hugh, dearest—are you afraid?" And his: "Trust me, little darling. Love me." A kiss.

Then a sharp, whispered summons: "Quick, can't you, Pete? Get these boards down."

When Pete turned, Hugh had dropped into the darkness, and Sylvie stood flushed and with her hands over her face.

Bella had meantime been collecting the most characteristic of Hugh's belongings—those that could not be supposed to belong to Pete—and now thrust them down into the hiding-place. The boards were rearranged, the rug laid evenly over them. Then the three stood staring at one another, listening helplessly to the nearing sounds.

"Oh, Pete," Sylvie gasped, "tell me what I must do—or what I ought to say."

"Tell them," said Bella, "what Hugh told you—that you are Pete's wife. They'll be looking for a different household from that, and it will help to put them off."

"But—but Pete won't look old enough."

"Yes, he will. He looks older than you," Bella declared harshly. "You sit down and keep quiet; that's the best you can do; and for God's sake don't look so scared. There's a grave outside to show them, and nobody digs up a six-year-old grave. They won't find Hugh. Nobody's ever seen him. Don't shake so, Sylvie. They may not even be after him; this country has sheltered other outlaws, you know. Hush! I hear them. I'll be in the kitchen. Pete, be taking off your outdoor clothes. They'll have seen Hugh's tracks even if they haven't seen him, so somebody's got to have just come in. Be whistling and talking, natural and calm. Remember we're all at home, just quiet and happy—no reason to be afraid. That's it."

Through her darkness Sylvie heard the knocking and Pete's opening of the door, the scraping of snow, the questions, the simplicity of Pete's replies.

Then she was made known. "My wife, gentlemen!" And a moment later: "My mother!" And she heard Bella's greeting, loud and cheerful like that of a woman who is glad to see a visitor. Chairs were drawn up and cigarettes rolled and lighted. She smelt the sharp sweetness of the smoke. There was brief talk of the weather; Sylvie felt that while they talked, the two strangers searched the place and the faces of its inmates with cold, keen, suspicious eyes. She was grateful now for her blindness. There came a sharp statement:

"We're looking for Ham Rutherford, the murderer." Sylvie's heart contracted in her breast.

"Well, sir," laughed Pete, in his most boyish, light-hearted fashion, "that sounds interesting. But it's a new name to me."

"It's an old case, however," said the man, the man who spoke more like an Easterner than the sheriff. "Fifteen years old! They've dug it up again back East. The daughter of the man that was killed came into some money and thinks she can't spend it any better than in hunting down her father's murderer. Now, we've traced Rutherford to this country, and pretty close to this spot. He made a getaway before trial, and he came out here fifteen years ago. About two years later he sent back East for his kid brother—he'd be about your age now, Mr.—what you say your name was?—Garth, Peter Garth. You'll have to excuse the sheriff; he's bound to search your place." Sylvie had heard the footsteps going through the three rooms. "A woman named Bertha Scrane, a distant cousin of Rutherford's to whom he'd been kind, brought the child out. Now, Missis—what's your name?"

"Bella Garth," she said tranquilly. "I came out here with my husband, who died six years ago. He's buried out there under the snow. I've lived here with my son and my son's wife."

"Yes. It's not the household we'd been expecting to find. It's a lonely place, Missis." He looked at Sylvie. "I should think you'd prefer going to some town."

"We're used to it here now," Bella answered.

"How'd your husband happen here, ma'am?"

"His health was poor; he'd heard of this climate, and he wanted to try trapping. He got on first-rate until the illness came so bad on him, and Pete's done well ever since. We haven't suffered any."

"No, I guess not. You don't look like you'd suffered."

The talk went on, an awkward, half-disguised cross-questioning as to Bella's birthplace, her life before she came out, her husband's antecedents. She was extraordinarily calm, ready and reasonable with her replies.

"Well, sir"—the sheriff strolled back into the room—"I reckon these aren't the parties we're after. But look a-here, this is a description of Ham Rutherford. Likely you might have had a glimpse of him since you came into the country. When he made his getaway he was about thirty-two, height five feet eight, ugly, black-haired, noticeable eyes, manner violent. He was deformed, one leg shorter, one shoulder higher than the other, mouth twisted, and a scar across the nose. He'd been hurt in a fire when he was a child—"

Sylvie broke into a spontaneous ripple of mirth, the full measure of her relief. "Goodness," she said with utter spontaneity. "There's certainly never been a monster like that in this house, has there, Pete?"

It did more than all that had gone before to convince the inquisitors. From that minute there was a distinct relaxation; the evening, indeed, turned to one of sociability.

"We hate to inconvenience you, ma'am, but it seems like at this distance from town we've got to ask you for supper and a place to sleep."

If it had not been for the thought of Hugh in hiding, that supper and the evening about the hearth would have been to Sylvie a pleasant one. The men, apparently laying aside all suspicion, were entertaining; their adventurous lives had bristled with exciting, moving, humorous experience. It was Sylvie herself, prompted by curiosity, believing as she did that the monster the sheriff had described bore no possible resemblance to the man she loved, who asked suddenly:

"Do tell us about the man you're hunting for now—this Rutherford? Tell us about what he did."

The Easterner gave her a look, and Bella, seeing it, chimed in: "Yes, sure. Tell us about his crime."

Pete stood up and rolled another cigarette. Try as he might to steady his fingers, they trembled. He had never heard Hugh's story. He did not want to hear it. The very name of Rutherford that had, in what now seemed to him another age, belonged to Hugh and to him was terrible in his ears. A sickness of dread seized him. Fortunately the eyes of neither of the men were upon him. Sylvie had their whole attention.

The detective spoke. "He was a storekeeper back in a university town, way East, where I came from. He kept a bookshop and had a heap of book-learning. I remember him myself, though I was a youngster. He was a wonderful, astonishing sort of chap, though as ugly as the devil; had a great gift of narration, never told the truth in his life, I guess, but that only made him all the more entertaining. And he had a temper—phew! Redhot! He'd fly out and storm and strike in all directions. That's what did for him. Some fool quarrel about a book it was, and the man, a frequenter of the shop, a scholar, a scientist, professor at the university, accused Rutherford of lying. Rutherford had a heavy brass paper-cutter in his hand. The professor had a nasty tongue in his head. Well, a tongue's no match for a paper-cutter. The professor said too much, called Rutherford a hump-backed liar and got a clip on the head that did for him."

"It's an ugly story," said Sylvie. Bella and Pete retained their silence.

"Murder ain't pretty telling, as a general thing," remarked the sheriff.

"No, though I've heard of cases where a man was justified in killing another man—I mean to save some one he loved from dreadful suffering," Sylvie replied.

"Well, ma'am, I don't know about that. I've read stories that make it look that way, but in all my experience, it's the cowards and the fools that kill, and they do it because they're lower down, closer to the beast, or perhaps to an uncontrolled child, than most of us."

"But there was a time," Bella said, with a smothered passion, "when an insult to a gentleman's honor had to be avenged."

"Yes, ma'am," drawled the sheriff, "in them history days things was fixed up to excuse animal doin's, kind of neater and easier and more becomin' than they are now. Well, Mr. Garth, can we have our beds? We've kept these ladies up talkin' long enough. Your mother looks plum wore out."

They slept in the bed usually shared by Pete and Hugh. Pete lay on the floor in the living-room not far from his brother's hiding-place—lay there rigid and feverish, staring at the night. Sylvie, at Bella's side, slept no better. Her imagination went over and over the story of Ham Rutherford's crime. She saw the little dark bookshop, the professor's thin, sneering face, the hideous anger of the cripple, the blow, the dead body, Rutherford's arrest. And when her brain was sick, it would turn for relief to the noble story of Hugh's self-sacrifice, only to be balked by a sense of unreality. What the detective had told, briefly and dryly, lived in her mind convincingly; but Hugh's romance, that had glowed on his tongue, now lay lifeless on her fancy. Back her mind would go to the bookshop, the gibing professor, the heavy paper-cutter.

In the dawn she heard Bella get up with a deep-shaken sigh and go about her preparations for breakfast. But it was noon before the two men left.

CHAPTER VIII

Hugh came up from his hiding-place like a man risen from the dead. They helped him to his chair before the fire; they poured coffee down him, rubbed his blue, stiff hands. He sat looking up pitifully, his eyes turning from one to the other of them like those of a beaten hound. All the masterfulness, all the bombast, had been crushed out of him; even the splendor of his flaring hazel eyes was dimmed—they were hollow, hopeless, old. For a long time he did not speak, only drank the coffee and submitted himself meekly to their ministrations; then at last he touched Sylvie with a trembling hand.

"Sylvie," he whispered brokenly.

"Hugh, dear, you're safe now; please speak; please laugh; you frighten me more than anything—why is he so silent, Pete? Bella, tell me what's wrong?"

"He's been crouching there on the damp, cold ground for hours," said Bella, "not knowing what might happen." Her voice trembled; she passed a hand as shaking as her voice across Hugh's bent head. "You're safe now. You're safe now," she murmured.

Hugh's teeth chattered, and he bent closer to the fire.

"Ugh it was cold down there," he said, "like a grave! Sylvie, come here." Just an echo of his old imperious fashion it was—though the look was that of a beggar for alms. "Give me those warm little hands of yours." She knelt close to him, rubbed his hands in hers, looking up at Pete with a tremulous mouth that asked for advice.

"He'll be all right in a minute," said Pete. "You talk to him, Sylvie."

"Yes, you talk—you talk. Do you remember how I talked to you when you were afraid of the bears—ah!" He drew her head savagely against his breast, folded his arms about it, stroked the hair. "Sylvie! Is it all right? Can it be—the same?"

"Yes, yes, why not?"

"Were you frightened?"

"Not after the first. After they had described you, I knew that they were looking for the wrong man, and then I felt all right. I didn't know—poor Hugh!—how cold and cramped you were. What a shame that you took a false alarm and hid yourself! I don't believe there would have been a bit of danger if you'd stayed out. They'd never even heard of you, I suppose."

Her talk, so gay, so strangely at cross-purposes with reality, was like a vivifying wine to him. The color came back into his face; a wild sort of relief lighted his eyes.

"Then it didn't occur to you, Sylvie, that that brute might have been me—that the men might, after all, have been describing me—eh?" he asked, risking all his hope on one throw.

She laughed, and, lifting herself a little in his arms, touched her soft mouth to his. "But, Hugh, you told me your story, don't you remember? And it is gloriously, mercifully different from Rutherford's."

He put his chin on his fist and stared over her head into the fire. She felt the slackening of his embrace and searched his arms with questioning fingers. "Why are you cross, Hugh? Did I say anything to hurt you? Let's forget Ham Rutherford. I wonder where he is, poor, horrible wretch!"

"Dead—dead—dead," Hugh muttered. "Dead and buried—or he ought to be. O God!" he groaned, and crushed her close against him; "I can't ask you to love me, Sylvie—to marry me. Now you know what it is like to love a man who must be afraid of other men. What right have I to ask any woman to share my life?"

"But, Hugh—if I love you?"

"And you do love me?" he asked.

"Yes."

He laughed out at that, stood up, drawing her to stand beside him. "Bella—Pete," he called, "do you hear—you two?" He beckoned them close, laid a hand on them, drew first one, then the other toward Sylvie. "She loves me. She sees me as I am!" Suddenly he put his grizzled head on Sylvie's shoulder and wept. She felt her way back to the chair, sat down, and drew him to kneel with his arms about her, her head bent over him, her small hands caressing him. She looked at Pete for help, for explanations, but she could not see his pale, tormented face.

After a while Hugh was calm and sat at her feet, smoking. But he was unnaturally silent, and his eyes brooded upon her haggardly.

It was several days before Hugh regained his old vigor and buoyancy; then it came to life like an Antaeus flung down to mother earth. His hour of doubt, of self-distrust, of compunction, was whirled away like an uprooted tree on the flood of his happiness. He flung reason and caution to the four winds; he dared Bella or Pete to betray him, he played his heroic part with boisterous energy; his tongue wagged like a tipsy troubadour's. What an empty canvas, a palette piled with rainbow tints, a fistful of clean brushes would be to an artist long starved for his tools, such was Sylvie's mind to Hugh. She was darkness for him to scrawl upon with light; she was the romantic ear to his romantic tongue; she was the poet reader for his gorgeous imagery. He had not only the happiness of the successful lover, but even more, the happiness of the successful creator. What he was creating was the Hugh that might have been.

With Sylvie clinging to his hand, he now went out singing—the three of them together, great Hugh and happy artist Hugh all but welded into one man for her and for her love. Those were splendid days, days of fantastic happiness. Hugh's joy, his sense of freedom, gave him a tenfold gift of fascination.

Yet one day—one of those dim, moist spring days more colorful to Hugh's heart than any of his days—there cut into his consciousness like a hard, thin edge, a sense of a little growing change in Sylvie. It had been there—the change,—slightly, dimly there, ever since the sheriff's visit. It was not that she doubted Hugh—such a suspicion would have struck him instantly aware and awake—but that she had become in some way uncertain of herself, restless, depressed, afraid. And it was always his love-making that brought the reaction, a curious, delicate, inner recoil, so delicate and slight, so deep beneath the threshold of her consciousness, that in the blind glory of his self-intoxication he missed it altogether—might, indeed, have gone on missing it, as she would have gone on ignoring or repressing it, if it had not been for their kiss on the mountain-top.

This was one of Hugh's madnesses; he would take Sylvie up a mountain and show her his kingdom, show her himself as lord of the wilderness. He had been there before many times, to the top of their one mountain, always under protest from Bella and Pete. It was a bare rock exposed to half the world and all the eyes of Heaven; and for a man in hiding, a man who lived, yet whose name was carved above a grave, it was a very target for untoward accident. Some trader or trapper down in the forest might look up and behold the misshapen figure black and bold, against the sky. Yet there was never so mighty a Hugh as when he stood there defiant and alone. Now he wanted Sylvie to sense that tragic magnificence.

So they went out, Hugh's arm about her, as strange a pair of lovers as ever tempted the spring—the great, scarred, uncouth, gray cripple and the slim, unseeing girl, groping and clinging, absolutely shut off from any contact with reality as long as this man should interpret creation for her. Sylvie turned back to wave at Pete, whom they had left standing in the doorway.

"I'll be hunting for you if you stay out late," he called—to which Hugh shouted back: "You hunting for us! Don't fancy I can't take care of this child, myself."

"Both of them blind!" Pete muttered to himself in answer.

They were moving rather slowly across the rough, sagebrush-covered flat, and presently Hugh led Sylvie into the fragrant silence of the forest trail. To her it was all scent and sound. Hugh whispered to her what this drumming meant and that chattering and that sudden rattle almost under their feet.

They had to go slowly, Sylvie touching the trees here and there, along her side of the trail. He lifted her over logs and fallen trees, and sometimes, before he set her down, he kissed her. Then Sylvie would turn her head shyly, and he would laugh. Thus they made slow, sweet progress.

"I see more in the woods with your eyes than I ever could with my own," she told him.

"I have eyes for us both," he answered. "That's why God gave me the eyes I have, because He knew the use I'd be making of them."

"Is this the trail Pete follows to the trading-station?" she asked. "I wish you could take me there, Hugh, or—would you let him take me?"

He tightened his arm. "I can't bear to have you out of my sight," he answered.

She sighed. "It seems so queer that they haven't tried to find me. Do you suppose they think that I'm dead? Did Pete mail my letter to Miss Foby, I wonder?"

"What does Miss Foby matter?" he asked jealously. "What does anything matter to you but—me? Here we leave Pete's trail and I take you straight up the mountain, dear one. We'll rest now and then; when we get to the rocky place just below the top, I'll carry you. Are you happy? I always feel as if my heart melted with the snow when spring comes—a wild, free, tumbling feeling of softness and escape."

She sighed. "Yes—if only I could see. I miss my eyes out of doors more than in the house. Does snow-blindness really last so long? Perhaps it was the nervous shock and the exhaustion as much as the glare. I am sure it all will just go suddenly some day. I stare and stare sometimes, and I feel as if I might see—almost."

He frowned. "You mustn't miss anything when you have me, Sylvie. Do you suppose I miss anything, now that I have you? My career, my old friends, my old life, my liberty, the world? That for everything!" He snapped his fingers. "If only I have you."

"You love me so much," she answered, as though she were oppressed, "it frightens me sometimes."

"When you are wholly mine—" he began. "Well, wait till we get to the top of the mountain; there I'll tell you all my plans. They're as big and beautiful as the world. I feel, with your love, that I can move mountains. I can fashion the world close to my heart's desire. We'll leave this blank spot and go to some lovely, warm, smiling land where the water is turquoise and the sky aquamarine—"

"And perhaps my sight will come back." It was almost a prayer.

He did not answer. They had come to a sharp sudden ascent. He took her in his arms, scrambled across the tumbled rocks, and set her down beside him on the great granite crest that rose like the edge of a gray wave. The clean, wild wind smote her and shook her and pressed back her hair and dress. She clung to him.

"Is it steep? Are we on the edge of a cliff, Hugh? I'm not afraid!"

"We're on the very top of the world," he told her breathlessly, his voice filled with a sense of awe, "our world, Sylvie, I'm master here. There's no greater mind than my own in all that dark green circle. It's pines, pines, pines to the edge of the earth, Sylvie, an ocean of purple and green—silver where the wind moves, treading down, like Christ walking on the water. And the sky is all gray, like stone."

"Can you see the flat, the cabin?"

"The flat, yes—a round green spot, way down there behind us. The cabin? No. That's in a hollow, you may be sure, well out of sight. I'm an outlaw, dearest, remember. There's a curve of the river, like a silver elbow. And Sylvie, up above us, an eagle is turning and turning in a huge circle. He thinks he's king. But, Sylvie, it's our world—yours and mine. This is our marriage."

She drew back. "What do you mean?"

"Haven't you a feeling for such images? We'll go before a parson—don't be afraid. Would I frighten you, Sylvie? I love you too much for that. Why, Sylvie, what's wrong?"

When his lips, clinging and compelling, had left hers, she bent her face to his arm and began to cry.

"Oh, I don't know. I don't know.... But please don't kiss me like that, not like that!"

He released her and half turned, but her hands instantly hunted for him, found him and clung.

"Hugh, don't be angry. Be patient with me. Try to understand. Perhaps it's because I am in the dark. I do love you. I do. But you must wait. Soon it will be spring for me, too. You don't understand? You're angry? But I can't explain it any better."

"You can lay your hand on me," he said hoarsely. "God knows I'm real enough." And he thought so! "My love for you is here like a granite block, Sylvie."

"I know. It is the one thing in the darkness that is real. I know you— your love, splendid and strong and brave. Wait just a little, Hugh. Try to be patient. Suddenly it will all come right. The fog will lift. Then we'll really be on top of the mountain." She laughed, but rather sadly.

"I will always hate this mountain-top," he said. "I used to love it. I was so close to happiness, and now you've snatched it out of my reach." He drew in sobbing breaths.

"No—it's myself I'm keeping from happiness, not you," she answered. "I know it will come right, but you must not hurry me. Dear Hugh, be patient." She found his hand and raised it, a dead weight, to her lips. "Please be patient. Let's go down out of this wind. I can't see your world, and I'm cold."

So, in silence—a dull gray silence Hugh led her down into the valley.

CHAPTER IX

They came down the hill rapidly and carelessly. Hugh, stung by pain and anger, threw himself over the rocks, and Sylvie was too proud to show her timidity or to ask for help. She crept and climbed up and down, saving herself with groping hand, letting one foot test the distances before she put the other down. At last the rattle of his progress sounded so far below that she quavered: "Aren't you going to wait for me, Hugh?"

He stopped short, and for a moment watched her silently; then, smitten by the pathos of her progress—a little child, she seemed, against the mountain toppling so close behind her—he came swinging up to her and gave her his hand.

"You *need* me, anyway, don't you?" he asked with a tender sort of roughness.

She couldn't answer because she didn't want him to know that he had made her cry. She kept her face turned from him and hurried along at his side.

"Why do you go so fearfully fast?" she was forced at last to protest.

"Because I want to get down from this accursed mountain. I want to get down into the woods again where I was happy."

"Hugh"—she pulled at his arm—"you are only a child after all."

"Perhaps."

"Well—" She stopped. "Go home alone, then. I'll be no worse off than when you found me the first time. Pete will come out and hunt for me. He has a far sweeter temper than you, Hugh, and doesn't think only of himself."

He swung away at that, resting his hand against a big rock to clear a hole; then, seeing her about to step down into it, he pivoted back, caught her up bodily in his arms, and, laughing, ran with her down the hill, bounding over the rocks, leaping over the crevices, while she clung to him in fright.

"You silly child!" he cried. "This is the way I'll take you home. Now I've got you, and I'll punish you well, too." She clung to him and begged him to stop. She was frightened by their rash, plunging progress, by his speech. She struggled. "Let me down. I won't be carried like this against my will. Hugh, let me down!"

"All right!" He fairly flung her from him on a grassy spot. He was about to leave her when a rushing rattle sounded above them. The boulder he had twice used to turn his own weight upon was charging down the hillside! Just in time he caught Sylvie, threw her to one side and fell prone, helpless, in the path of the slide. He cried out, flinging up his arm, and, as though his cry had been of magic, the boulder faltered and stopped. A root half buried just above his body had made a hollow and a ledge; it had rocked the rolling fragment back up on its haunches, so to speak, and balanced it to a stop.

"Hugh! Hugh!" sobbed Sylvie. "What was it? Are you hurt?"

She crept up to him.

"No," Hugh told her, breathing heavily. "It was a rolling rock."

"How did you stop it? You must be hurt, crushed, bruised."

"My arm's wrenched—not badly." He had in fact wrenched it slightly.

"Your poor arm! You were so quick, so strong. You didn't think of your own life. And I've been so cruel. Hugh, Hugh, kiss me."

Hugh took his reward, none the less sweet to his strange nature, in that it was only potentially earned. And joy, like a warm flood, crept up again to his heart. He sat on the hillside and held his small love close. One of his arms moved stiffly, and he groaned a little. She rubbed it for him.

"You'd better come home and let Bella and me fix it. It may be badly hurt. You're sure it isn't broken?" she asked.

"Quite sure."

"Lean on me! I'll help you down. You can tell me where to step."

"Nonsense," he laughed, his very blood singing warm with relief. "A strained arm won't hurt my walking apparatus. We had a lover's quarrel, didn't we? And the boulder was peacemaker. Bless the boulder!"

"Don't joke, dear. You saved my life at the risk of your own. Are you always doing insane, generous, dangerous things? Think if you had been—" She shivered.

"Do you suppose my life is worth anything to me without yours, Sylvie?" He bent his head and kissed her again, but he had learned his lesson, and there was restraint and timidity in that kiss.

"The sun's come out," cried Sylvie.

"Yes, it's splendidly bright. There's a clean slit in the sky; there at the western edge the dark gray cap is being lifted inch by inch, the way a boy lifts his cap to see the butterfly he's caught. All's gold behind it, Sylvie, burning gold. The rocks are like bright copper. And the pines, they're incandescent, phosphorescent green—"

"If I could only see it!"

Down near the pines a tall, still figure stood watching them. It was Pete, and his smile, usually so frank and sweet, had now a sardonic twist. As they came down out of their sun into his shadow, he spoke with a drag to his syllables.

"Hullo," he said. "That was a narrow escape you had, you two!"

The voice might have been a pistol-shot for the start it gave to Hugh.

"Why, it's Pete. We must be late, Pete," Sylvie called joyously. "Did you see how Hugh saved my life? He threw himself down before the rock and stopped it. He's hurt his poor arm. The great stone was right on top of us, and he threw me out of the way and set his own strength against it. I couldn't see the rock, Pete, but it felt like a mountain."

"It was big enough to smash you both," said Pete.

He looked at Hugh, whose eyes glared in a strained, shamed face. The older man's fingers worked nervously; he opened his lips and closed them again. It was easy to understand the travail of his mind, unwilling to forego the imaginary bit of heroism, and yet abashed by the boy's awareness of the lie.

Pete gave one short laugh; then, springing suddenly across a fallen tree that separated them, he caught Sylvie up into his arms.

"You can't carry her with a wrenched arm," he said, half gayly, half tauntingly, "and at the best rate she can go, it will be night before we get her home. I'm strong. I'll carry her myself."

Sylvie laughed protesting that she was being treated like a doll, and resigned herself to Pete's swift, smooth stride. It was as though she were skimming through space, so quietly did his moccasined feet press the pine-needled earth, so exquisitely did his young strength save her from any jar. He whistled softly through his teeth as he ran in long, swift strides. And as he did not speak to her, she lay silent, yet strangely peaceful and happy. Hugh was left far behind. The forest fragrance moved cool and resinous against her face.

"I feel as if we could go on and on forever," she said with a sigh, "forever and ever and ever."

"We will," he answered through his teeth, hardly pausing in his whistling for the odd reply. "We will."

But for all that, he set her gently and suddenly down, and she knew that she stood again at the cabin door.

"Pete, where are you?" she asked.

But he had disappeared, still in utter silence, like a genie whose task is done.

CHAPTER X

"What did he say to you? What did he say to you?" asked Hugh again and again.

Sylvie laughed at him.

"He didn't say anything—hardly a word, except that he pretended he was going on forever. He said: 'We will, we will.' That's absolutely all, Hugh. Don't be so silly. What *could* he say?"

"I don't know," Hugh answered. "He might have made fun of me."

"Fun of you! After saving my life! I'd have boxed his ears! No, no, Peter wouldn't do that. He's afraid of me."

She was so proud of this that Hugh, perforce, laughed. It was after supper, and they had walked a little way from the cabin. They were standing just above the river on a little hillock topped with three big pines. The dusk was thick about them; stars pricked the soft sky. Sylvie was wrapped in Hugh's coat, and they were linked by their hands hanging at their sides. Every one but Sylvie had been very silent at supper, but she had told her story of Hugh's heroism again and again until finally even Hugh had grumbled at "the fuss."

"What makes you think anyone could be afraid of you?" He smiled down at the small dark head which did not reach his shoulder.

"He's afraid I'll kiss him. Don't grip my hand that way; it hurts. You couldn't be jealous of a boy! Besides, I *don't* kiss him any more. I never have kissed him but that once—no, twice, when I told him that I was going to be his sister."

"You told him that?" Hugh's voice had an odd anxiety. "How did he take it?"

"I don't think he was very enthusiastic. He loves you so much, Hugh; you are the very heart of his universe, and I suppose he is jealous of your love for me. Since then he's avoided me and is as dumb as a fish when I talk to him. I think his body has outgrown his mind, Hugh."

"Perhaps. I don't know," he answered.

"And Bella is so silent, too. Hugh, it must have been a lonely life for you before I came. Those two people, though they love you so much, are not companionable. I think, Hugh, that they aren't able to understand you. You are so brilliant, and they are so dull; you are so articulate, and they are so dumb; you are so warm, so quick to see, to feel, to sympathize, while they are so slow and so cold. Dear Hugh, I'm glad I came. I am stupid myself, but I have enough intelligence to understand you—a little, haven't I, dear?"

"So much more than enough!" The low speech with its tremor of humility was almost lost.

"What a noise the river makes!" he said presently.

"Yes. And the pines. The whole air is full of rushing and sighing and clapping and rattling. Sounds tell me so much now. They fill my whole life. It is very queer. Why, a voice means more to me now, I think, than a face ever did.... Is it a deep river, Hugh?"

"Now it is—deep and dangerous. But it goes down very quickly when the snow at its source has melted. In summer it is a friendly little brook, and in the fall a mere trickle that hardly wets your shoe. I have a boat here tied to the root of one of these trees, a boat I made myself, to pole across when the stream is too deep for wading. I'll take you out in it when the flood's down; it wouldn't last fifteen minutes now. In the spring, Sylvie, a nymph comes down from the mountain, a wild white nymph. She has ice-green hair and frost-white arms; you can see her lashing the water, and if you listen, you can hear her sing and cry. Let's go in, dear; you're tired and cold—I can feel you shivering. We'll start a big fire, and I'll tell you how that nymph caught me once and nearly strangled me with her cold, wet arms. I was trying to save—you'll laugh when I tell you about it—a baby bear."

Pete and Bella made room for them silently about the hearth where Pete had already built up a fire. Sylvie groped her way to the throne from which the other woman slipped half furtively and so noiselessly that Sylvie never guessed her usurpation.

"Hugh is going to tell us a story," she said, and rested her head back so that her small chin pointed out and her slim neck was drawn up—"a wonderful story about the river and a bear. I hope it's a baby bear, Hugh, for you know how I feel about bears. I honestly think that being so afraid of seeing them is what made me blind!" She gave her small, shy laugh. "I thought I saw them everywhere I looked that day and night. It seems so long ago now, and yet it is not so many weeks. I can still hear Hugh's voice calling out to me across the snow. And now," she said, "the snow's all gone and none of you are strangers any more, and—Go on with your story, Hugh."

Pete added a log to the fire so that the flames stretched up bravely and made a great fan of light against which they all seemed painted like ornamental figures, Hugh lounging along the rug to make a striking central figure. Bella was drawn up rigidly on a stiff, hard chair; she hemmed a long, coarse towel with her blunt, work-roughened fingers.

Pete sat opposite Sylvie on the floor, his back against the corner of the fireplace, his knees drawn up in his hands, his head a little bent. He too—from under his long level brows—looked for the most part at Hugh, not devotedly, not wistfully, but with a somber wondering. It was only now and then, and as though he couldn't help it, that the blue, smouldering Northern eyes were turned to Sylvie on her throne. Then they would brighten painfully, and his lips would tighten so that the dimple, meant for laughter, cut itself like a touch of pain into his cheek. The firelight heightened his picturesqueness—the dull blue of his shirt, open at the round, smooth throat, the dark gold-brown of his corduroy trousers, against which the long, tanned hands, knit strongly together, stood out in the rosy, leaping light—beautifully painted against the background of old brown logs.

Yet it was Hugh, after all, who dominated the room by right of his power, his magnetism, the very distortion of his spirit. Here in this lonely square of light and warmth, surrounded by a world of savage, lawless winds heightening the voices of vast loneliness, these three people were imprisoned by him, a Merlin of the West.

He sat up to begin his story, pressing tobacco into his pipe. "Oh, it's not so much of a story, Sylvie. It was last spring when the river was high and I'd been out with my traps. I was coming home along the river edge, pretty tired, a big load on my back. I came around a bend of the river, and not far below me a little black bear, round as a barrel, was trying to scramble over the flood on a very shaky log. The mother was on the other side, but I didn't know that then. Well, there's nothing in God's world, Sylvie, so beguiling as a baby bear. This little fellow was scared by what he was doing, but he was bound he'd get across the river. He'd make a few steps; then he'd back up and half rise on his hind legs. I watched him a long time. Then he made up his mind he'd better make a dash for it. He began scrambling like a frantic kitten, and it was just in the most ticklish spot that he heard me and jumped and went rolling off into the river. I tell you, my heart came right up into my mouth."

"Oh, *was* he drowned?" wailed Sylvie.

Hugh rose and stood with his back to the fire, dominating the room even more convincingly, with his vivid ugliness. Sylvie's face turned up to him like a white flower to the sun it lives by, without seeing. It was strange to watch the adoration, the worship on that small face, and at the same time to behold the grotesqueness toward which it was directed. Bella was listening with her lowered eyes and tightened lips. She was interested in spite of herself; and Pete's inscrutable face followed the story with absorption.

"Well, in he rolled with a splash and went rattling down the current, turning over and over. Like a fool, I threw away my hides, ran down the bank and jumped in after him—that is, I meant to hold on to a branch and stand out in the water and catch him as he went by. But the nymph I told you about had her own plans. She wrapped her arms round me, and away we went, bear all. Oh, yes, I'd caught the cub all right, and he was about half drowned by that time—no fight left in him.

"Well, for a bit it was a question whether the world wouldn't be quickly and well rid of us both, but we tumbled up against a root and scrambled out, and when I'd rested, I picked up limp and trembling Master Bear and went back for my hides. And while I was collecting them, I heard a sort of grumpy, grumbling sound, and I looked up—and, by Jove, Mother Bear was coming across that log with the longest steps you ever saw. That's when I ran to collect my gun—it was a little farther up the bank than my hides, worse luck!"

Even Bella had forgotten her bitterness in listening, and Pete's parted lips were those of an excited child. Sylvie leaned forward in her chair, her cheeks tingling, her hands locked. Hugh had thrown himself into the action of his story; his face was slightly contorted as though sighting along a gun-barrel, his arm raised, the ungainliness of his deformity strongly accentuated. He was not looking at Sylvie; true to his nature and his habit, he had forgotten every one but that Hugh of adventure and of romance, the one companion of his soul. None of them was watching Sylvie, and when she gave a sharp, little cry, a queer start and then sat utterly still, Hugh accepted it—they all accepted it—as a tribute to his story-telling powers.

But Sylvie, leaning her elbows on her knees, raised trembling hands to her eyes and hid them. She sat very still, very white, while the story went on, vividly imagined, picturesquely told. When it was over, and the mother bear, after a worthy struggle, defeated, Hugh looked about for his applause. It came, grudgingly from Bella, eagerly from Pete—and from Sylvie in a sudden extravagant clapping of hands, a ripple of high, excited laughter, and a collapse in her chair. She had fainted in a limp little heap.

She came to in an instant, but seemed bewildered and, unprotesting, permitted herself to be carried to bed. She declared she felt quite well again and wanted only to be alone. She repeated this moaningly. "Oh, to be alone!"

Hugh seated himself on the end of the bed and kissed her forehead and her hand, but it quivered under his lips and was drawn away.

He came back into the living-room with a pale, bewildered face.

CHAPTER XI

Next day there came out of that room a new Sylvie or rather a dozen new Sylvies: a flighty witch of a Sylvie who tempted her blindness with rash ventures about the rooms and even out of doors, who laughed at Hugh and led him on, and drew him out to his maddest improvisations, who treated Pete to snubs and tauntings that stung like so many little whips; and again a Sylvie who was still and timid and a trifle furtive, who rarely spoke, but sat with locked hands in an attitude of desperate concentration and seemed to be planning something secret and dangerous; and then there was a haughty, touch-me-not Sylvie; and a Sylvie who mysteriously wept. But all of these Sylvies showed an impetuous, new tenderness toward Bella.

"I've been all wrong about you, Bella," she confessed. "I know you're not really old and ugly and cross at all. Let me touch your face." Bella, awkward and flushed, had no choice but to submit to the flick of the light, young fingers. "I'm learning the touch of the blind," Sylvie boasted. "Now, listen—isn't this right? You have thick, straight eyebrows and deep-set eyes; are they blue or brown, Bella, or bright gray?"

"They're gray," said Pete.

Hugh was watching from eyes sunk in a nervous, pallid face. He had come in from his traps in the midst of Sylvie's experiment.

"And she has a nice, straight, strong, short nose, and a mouth that she holds too tight. Loosen your mouth, Bella; it might be very sweet if you gave it a chance. And she has a sharp chin—not pretty, your chin, but—look! If you'd soften your hair, pull it over your ears and forehead—Why do you brush it back that way? It *must* be unbecoming. And, Bella, it's curly, or would be with a little freedom. What color is your hair?"

"Gray—like my eyes," said Bella, scarlet now, and trying to draw herself away.

"Is it really gray, Pete? Tell me the truth, if you can."

"Her hair is a very light brown," said Pete, flushed as scarlet now as Bella; "sort of a grayish brown; you wouldn't notice any gray hairs, hardly."

"Bella, I'm sure you don't look a day older than thirty-five. Your skin feels smooth and young. Why do you let Hugh call you an old woman? Poor Bella, I'm afraid you've spoiled those two boys?"

Sylvie turned suddenly and imperiously upon the men, and Bella made her escape, not from the room, for she was too stirred, too full of an excited suspense, to bring herself to leave. From a far corner, near the window through which came the soft May wind, she watched them.

"Now, Pete," said Sylvie, "it's your turn. If I'm to learn the touch of the blind, I must have practice. What can I make of you! Come here. Why don't you come?" She stamped her foot. "My, but you are badly trained. Really, Hugh, you ought to discipline him. Wait until I am your sister-in-law."

Hugh started angrily. "Don't joke about that!" he threatened in a harsh, sudden voice.

She turned toward him with quickness and bent her head sidelong as though listening intently for what else he might have to say. Her lips were set close and narrow. She had listened to him like this, almost breathlessly, ever since her sudden faintness, listened as though she would draw his very soul in through her ears.

He too flushed. "It's life and death to me, Sylvie," he pleaded.

"Life and death—life *or* death," she repeated strangely. She stood, as if turning the speech over in her mind, then gave her head a quick little shake like a diver coming to the surface of deep water, and moved a step toward Pete. "Are you coming, boy, or not? I want to feel your face."

"Do as she says," Hugh commanded harshly, and Pete came slowly to her and stood with his hands locked behind him, bending over the little figure. She put her hands on his shoulders and gave him a shake, and smiled.

"Such a big, strong boy! Where's your face?" It winced and paled under her touch. His eyes fell, shifted, could not meet Hugh's, who watched with unsteady breathing and white lips.

"Your face is as smooth as a girl's, Pete. What a wide, low forehead and crisp, short hair; it ripples back from your temples. You must be a pretty boy! A neat nose and a round, hard chin and—oh, Pete, Pete! I believe you have a dimple. How absurd! A great, long dimple like a slit in your right cheek. Why do you blink your eyes so? They're long eyes, with thick, short lashes. What a strong, round neck! I think I like your face."

She patted his cheek, the pat more like a smart slap. He pulled away. "That's for disobedience. Come back. I'm not through with you. Where's your mouth? A big, long mouth. Pete, why does your mouth tremble?" Her hand fell from his lips, and she turned away. "Take me out for a walk, Hugh, please," she said. "This cabin is stuffy, now that the days are warm. I want to sit under the pines and listen to the river. You can tell me one of your wonderful stories about yourself."

"What does it mean, Bella?" Pete asked breathlessly when Hugh had gone out, not so much leading the girl as hurrying after her to save her from the rashness of her impetuous progress. "What does it mean?" Pete was as white as paper.

"I don't know." Bella came over from the window and stood by the fireplace, rolling her arms in her apron and shaking her head. "She's a crazy little witch. She'll drive us mad. Hugh is half mad now—have you noticed? She won't let him touch her. And you, poor boy! Pete, why don't you go away?"

"I've thought about it," he said. "I—I can't." He flung himself down in Hugh's chair and rested his head in his hands.

Bella bent over him. "Poor Pete! It's cruel for you—and," she added softly, uncertainly, "and for me."

"For you too, Bella?" He looked up at her through tears.

She nodded her head, and her face worked. "Perhaps you could take her back to her friends, Pete?"

"And leave Hugh? Didn't you hear what he said, Bella? Life and death! It would kill him if she should go away with me. Or—he'd follow and kill me."

"Yes," Bella assented somberly; "yes, he'd kill you. The devil is still living in his heart."

"No. Sylvie will marry him. Hugh gets his will." Pete shook his head. "Wait a few days—you'll see. She's fighting against him now; I don't know why—some instinct. But though he tells her so many lies, he doesn't lie about one thing. He loves her. He does love her."

"No! No!" Bella's passion, tearing its way through her long habit of repression, was almost terrifying. "He loves the image she has of him. If he knew that she could see him as I do, his love would shrivel up like a flower in a drought. Hugh can't love the truth. He can't love anything but his delusions. Pete, tell her the truth. For God's sake, tell her the truth. Give her back her eyesight. Let her know his name, his story—his *face!*"

"Don't dare ask me, Bella!"

"Why not?" She seemed to be out of breath, like a person who has been climbing in thin air. Her lips were dry.

"Because—well, would you do it yourself?"

"Ah! He would hate me, if I did. But you, Pete, when Sylvie loved you—and if she knew you, she would surely love you; any woman would—why, then you could bear Hugh's hatred. I have only him—only him."

She locked her hands and lifted them to her forehead and was now making blind steps toward the kitchen door.

Pete followed her, and turning her about, drew down the hands from her face.

"Bella—*you?* Without saying a word? All these years?"

Under the first pressure of sympathy that her agony had ever known, she could not speak. She bent her head for an instant against his arm, then moved away from him, groping through the kitchen door, back to her unutterable loneliness.

Pete stood staring after her. A new Bella, this, not the cousin, the little cousin from the farm; not the nurse who had saved him from Hugh's hardness and told him limping fairy tales and doctored his hurts; not the accepted necessity, but a woman—a woman young, yes, young. In the instant when he had glimpsed her face, broken and quivering, the tight lips parted and the hair disarranged about flushed, quivering cheeks, the eyes deep with widened pupils, she had revealed beauty and passion—the two halves of youth. How blind, how blind Hugh had been, blind and selfish and greedy, drinking up the woman's heart, feeding upon her youth!

CHAPTER XII

"When you sit so silent, Pete," Sylvie said softly, "I sometimes wonder if you're not staring at me."

"When I'm making a trap," he answered, smiling a little to himself and instinctively shifting his gaze, "I can't very well be staring at you, can I?"

He was kneeling on the ground before the cabin door, she sitting on the low step under the shadow of the roof. Her chin rested on the backs of her hands, the limber wrists bent up a little, the sleeves slipped away from her slim, white wrists. Her face was brightly rosy, her lips very red—at once a little stern, yet very sweet.

"Traps are cruel," she said.

"I think so myself. But we have to make a living, don't we?"

"Aren't you ashamed of yourself sometimes, Pete?"

"For making traps, and catching live things in them?"

"Yes. It's a sort of deceitful cruelty, catching the little blind, wandering wild things."

"Blind?" he repeated blankly, then flushed.

"Yes, blind. But it wasn't only that I meant."

"What else ought I to be ashamed of?"

"Of living on your brother." He winced sharply, but she went on coolly: "Of staying here in the wilderness. You are a big boy now. Many a boy of your age, even smaller and weaker, has gone out in the world to make his own way. There's no reason for *you* to hide, is there? *You* haven't sacrificed your life for anyone."

"No," he answered doubtfully, "n-no; but, you see, Sylvie, some one has to take the skins. It isn't safe for Hugh."

"Yes, of course. So that's what you'll do all your life—carry loads to and fro, between this cabin and the trading-station. But if Hugh goes away himself?"

"Yes?" he asked breathlessly.

His skillful hands paused in their fashioning of a snare.

"You know, of course, that he wants to take me away with him, to marry me, to start life again."

"And—and you will, Sylvie?"

"Give me your advice," she said. She pressed her red lips together; her face was bent upon him as though she watched.

"But," he stammered, "you tell me all the time, a dozen times a day, that I'm badly trained. What good's my advice?"

"*Are* you badly trained?"

"I suppose so."

"You are absurdly unselfish, Pete!" She moved a chip along the ground with her foot, but Pete failed to notice this curious seeing gesture.

"Why? What do you mean?"

She waited, waited until, in the sickness of his vague suspense, his hands had turned cold and the color had sucked itself in irregular heartbeats from his lips.

At last she spoke deliberately. "You would lay down your life for your friend?" she said. It was almost a whisper.

Pete's face went red and white and red again. Through the tumult of his heart he searched for loyal words.

"I love Hugh—if that's what you mean," he said.

"I love you?" she repeated softly, perversely. "Did you say 'Hugh' or 'you,' Pete?"

His face tightened; faint lines came about his mouth. "I said 'Hugh!'"

"Ah—you love only him—nobody else in all the world?"

Her young and wistful voice came to him like a fragrance. He struggled as though his spirit were fighting in deep water. He tried to remember Hugh. He rose up slowly to meet this passionate moment, and now he made a short step toward the waiting girl. She *was* waiting, breathing fast. Pete's arms quivered at his sides.

A hand gripped the quivering muscles and turned him about. Hugh had come up behind, without sound, on moccasined feet. His face was gray; his eyes were drawn into slits; his distorted mouth was trying to become a straight, hard line. The effort gave a twitch to the pale, lower lip.

Sylvie stood up, singing as though in absent-minded idleness, and vanished into the house. It would have been difficult to tell whether or not she had heard Hugh's arrival.

"What's the matter?" Pete stammered like a boy wakened from a dream to behold a lifted cane. "Let go my arm, Hugh. Your fingers cut."

"Come away from the house," said Hugh coldly, tightening the iron grip as though Pete's wincing gave him satisfaction. "Come up here by the pines. I want to talk to you."

"I'll come," said Pete. "Let go my arm."

There was that in his voice that compelled obedience. Hugh's hand fell and knotted into a fist. Pete walked beside him up the abrupt slope of their hollow to the little hill above the river. Its noise was loud in the still, sunny air. There was no wind stirring. It was high noon. A sloping tent of shadow drooped from the pines and made a dark circle about their roots. In this transparent, purplish tent the brothers faced each other. Pete's lips were tremulous, and Hugh's distorted.

"Now," said Hugh, breathing irregularly and speaking very low, "I'll tell you what I think of you."

"No, Hugh, don't," Pete pleaded. "You'll say things you don't mean—unkind things, terrible things. I don't deserve it from you. You—you think that I—that I—"

"Go on. Don't stop. Tell me what I think—I think—that you—that you—"

It was an unbearable moment, an impossible atmosphere, for the revelation of a first love. Pete felt stripped and shamed.

"You think that I was telling Sylvie, that Sylvie—that I—"

Hugh lifted his hand and struck. The younger man sprang back, then forward, and was at his elder's throat. For an instant they struggled, silently, terribly, slipping on the red pine-needles. Then Pete gave a hard laugh. "Are we tigers?" he asked, and he pulled himself back and leaned, shaking, against a tree-trunk, gripping it with his hands. His blue eyes were cold and blazing in his white face, against which Hugh's blow had made a mark. "You won't strike me again," Pete said. All boyishness was gone from his hard, level voice. "Go on. Say what you like. I'll listen."

"You liar!" stormed Hugh. "You cheat!"

Pete laughed again.

A certain quality in his bitter self-control flicked Hugh. He tried to emulate the young man's coolness.

"I've trusted you," he began again; "and behind my back you have been trying to win the love of the woman who has promised to be my wife."

"I have not."

"You were not making love to her there, then, when I came up behind you? When you were so excited that you didn't hear me? when you were moving toward her—trembling all over? *I* felt your arm!"

Pete's eyes dropped, then lifted as though under a great weight.

"And you say you're not a liar!"

"I *am* a liar, though not in the way you mean. We are all liars. We have caught that little blind girl in a trap. We have lied to her, all three of us—Bella and I, and you, Hugh—you have lied most of all."

"She loves me," Hugh panted. "She knows me. She understands me."

"Yes," Pete answered, trembling. "I've seen that. I've kept quiet. Bella and I have given you your happiness. Now you thank me by striking me and calling me a liar and a cheat!"

Hugh, even in the midst of his bitter and suspicious rage, felt the justice of the reproach. He paused, looked about, then came close, put a hand on each of his brother's shoulders, searching the white, young face with his wild eyes.

"I must have Sylvie," he groaned. "Pete, I must. You don't know; you can't know—" He dropped his grizzled head against Pete's neck, and his breath caught. "You don't know what I felt when I saw you there, when I thought—Tell me the truth, Pete. You are not going to take my love, my only joy, my one prize away from me?"

After a long and difficult silence Pete put his arm half mechanically across the twisted, gasping back.

"Of course not, Hugh. I—I couldn't. But I've had to play a part, and it's not come easy. You must have guessed how hard it's been, because you seem to have guessed how I—how Sylvie—Perhaps if I went away?"

He was gripped again, shaken a little. "No, don't leave me. Wait. It won't be long. She will go away with me soon, as soon as she gets over a girl's timidity. Pete, she does love me. She does. Don't stand dumb; tell me that she does."

"She does," Pete repeated tonelessly.

"I'm sorry I struck you. I have a devil's temper. And I think of you as still a boy. I wanted to beat you. A few years ago I would have beaten you." He put this forward as though it were a reasonable excuse.

"Yes." Pete smiled grimly. "I can remember your beatings." He drew himself away. "Shall we go back?"

Hugh still held him, though at arm's length. "First I must have a promise from you." He spoke sternly.

"What do you want?"

"I want your promise to keep hands off, to hold your tongue to the end."

"You won't trust me, then?"

"Not since I watched you moving toward her, not since I felt your arm."

Pete was silent. He studied the ground. There was a sullen look on his face, and his tightened mouth deepened the odd, incongruous dimple.

"Well, perhaps you're right. I promise." He flashed up a blue desperation of young eyes as he asked: "How long will it last, Hugh?"

"Not long. Not long. Surely not long."

"I promise."

"Give me your hand."

They came back down from the hill.

CHAPTER XIII

Pete looked forward with white-hot impatience to the day of his trip to the trading-station; twelve hours of relief, it would mean, from the worst pressure of his torment—twelve hours of merciful solitude in the old, voiceful friendliness of his forest trail. He started early, at the break of a sweet, singing dawn. The earth was elastic under his feet, the air tingling and mellow with a taste of growth; the flooded river chattered loudly like a creature half beside itself with joy. Pete came out of the dark and silent cabin in which he had made his tiptoe preparations, and lifted his face, letting the light, soft fingers of the wind, cooler and softer even than Sylvie's, smooth out the knots of suffering from his tired brain. He shook his shoulders before settling them under the load of pelts. He would, he swore, just for this day, be a boy again. He sprang lightly up from the hollow and strode forward with long, swift steps, swinging a companionable stick in his free hand.

Loneliness and the dawn and love had made a poet of the young man, so that he had the release of poetry and forgot reality in its translation into a tale that is told. He thought of Sylvie, but he thought of her as a man thinks of a lovely memory. He went through the wood with his chin lifted, half smiling, almost happy, an integral part of the wild, glad, wistful spring.

It was not until the afternoon when he was nearing the station—just, in fact, before he left the wood-trail for the rutted, frontier road—that his mind was caught as sharply as a cloth by a needle, by the light sound of following steps. In the solitude of that trail which his feet alone had worn, the sound brought him to a stop with a sense of terror and suspense. His mind leaped to Hugh, and for the first time in his loyal life Pete remembered, and remembering, felt a creeping on his skin, that this brother of his, who had grown harsh and jealous and suspicious, had been a murderer. The cold, unkindly memory slid along his senses like a snake. On the edge of the sloping road-bank, studded with little yellow flowers, just where the trees stopped, Pete set down his load and waited, instinctively bracing his body, drawing it back beneath the shelter of one of the big pines.

The steps were light and swift and stealthy. In the purplish confusion of the distance, a tangled and yet ordered regiment of trunks and boughs, sun-splotches and shadow-blots, through which the uncertain trail seemed to rise like a slender thread of smoke to the pale, flecked sky, Pete made out a moving shape. It slipped in and out; it hesitated, hurried, paused, moved on. With a shudder of relief and of surprise, Pete saw it; out from behind the great, close trunks came Sylvie, her chin lifted, her hands stretched out on either side, brushing the swinging branches along the trail, her small head turning from this side to that, as though she listened in suspense.

Pete called out her name and ran quickly to meet her. Forgetting his part of a dull, sullen boy, he spoke eagerly, catching her hand, watching the warm, happy blush flow in her cheeks.

"Where were you?" she asked. She had stood to wait for him as soon as his voice reached her. "I couldn't see—I mean, I lost the sound of your steps. I've been following you for hours and hours and hours. I was so afraid of being lost again that I didn't dare drop too far behind."

"But why didn't you call to me? Why have you come? Is anything wrong at home?"

Her fingers moved uncertainly in his grasp, like the fingers of a shy child. "Nothing is wrong. I wanted to come with you. I wanted to go to the trading-station and the post-office. I didn't dare ask you to take me with you. I was afraid you'd send me home. I suppose I'll be a nuisance, but— Oh, Pete, please be nice to me and take care of me, won't you?" She paused, turned her face away from him and smiled. "After all, since you have called me your wife before witnesses, you ought to introduce me to your friends at the trading-station, oughtn't you? They might think it was queer that I should hide myself, now that the snow has gone."

He dropped her hand. Suddenly he realized the consequences, the necessary effect upon Hugh of this willful venture of hers.

"Does Hugh know where you are?" he asked painfully.

"No. I ran away. I heard you getting ready, and I just felt that I couldn't bear to be left behind. I slipped out of bed so quietly that Bella didn't even stir, and I dressed just as quietly, and when you had gone half across the clearing, I ran out after you, listening to your steps. You see, I have the hearing, as well as the touch, of the blind." This was said with a cunning sort of recklessness; but Pete, absorbed in his anxiety, did not challenge the improbable statement. "Please don't be angry with me, Pete." She touched his hand where it hung at his side. "Can't I have my adventure? Let's call it *ours*."

In spite of himself, the young man's pulse quickened, but his face and voice were stern.

"Do you know that we'll be very late?" he said. "It will be midnight before we can possibly make it back to the cabin, if you can even do it at all. You'll have to spend the night somewhere at the station. What will they think? They will be anxious, Bella and Hugh."

"But what can they think?" Her cheeks were unexplainably scarlet. "If I choose to trust you to take care of me, why should they grumble? And I won't have to spend the night. You don't know how strong I am. I'm very strong. I don't feel tired. We'll go back by moonlight. There's a beautiful moon."

"It will be almost morning." He made a reckless gesture. "Well, it's too late to think of that now. Come on."

He threw himself down the bank, held up his hands to catch hers, and swung her down beside him. The sun slanted warmly along the road and just ahead flickered the blue ripples of a lake.

Sylvie moved quickly and easily beside him, barely touching his arm with her hand. She seemed definitely to decide to put away her childishness. She treated him as though she had forgotten his supposed youth; she talked straightforwardly, with a certain dignity, about her childhood, about her amusing and pitiful experience as a third-rate little actress, and she asked him a question now and then half diffidently, which he answered in stumbling, careful speech, always weighed upon by his promise, by the deception he must practice, by the dread of what must come. Nevertheless, minute by minute, his pulse quickened. This, God be thanked, would mean the end. The insufferable knot of circumstance, so fantastic, so extravagantly unlivable and unreal, would break, Hugh would tear the tangle of his making to tatters with angry hands when they got back. His difficult trust in Pete's promise would go down under the strain of these long and unexplained hours of Sylvie's absence in his company. It was the last act in the extravaganza, queer and painful, that had twisted them all out of their real shapes for the confusion of a blind waif. This adventure that Sylvie's impatience had planned would bring down the curtain. After all, no matter what came of it, Pete was glad. The color warmed his face; his blue eyes deepened; he smiled down at Sylvie beside him. For this hour she seemed to belong to him rightfully, naturally, by her own will. He let go of his inhibitions and resigned himself to Fate.

When, on the far shore of the lake, the low walls of the trading-station came in sight, a double image, reflected faithfully with the strip of sand at its door, the low, level wall of pines behind and the blue, still sky above, Pete caught the girl's hand in his.

"Here we are, Sylvie," he said. "Keep quiet and follow my lead. Remember, now, that I am supposed to be your husband and you my wife. Can you play that part?"

She nodded, bending down her face so that he saw only the tip of her small, sunburnt chin. She was hatless; the sun struck blue, bright lines in her black hair.

"I'll be careful, Pete."

She pressed his hand, and he returned the pressure.

The station was full of silent curiosity; a couple of squaws, a serious buck Indian, and a bearded trapper or two made little secret of their observation. In the far corner of the big, bare room, down one side of which ran a long and littered counter, there was another, even more interested spectator of the young couple's entrance. He sat at a small table under one of the high, unshaded windows, and from over a spread-out time-table he gave them a large and heavy share of his attention. He was a man of middle age and sturdy build, round, clean-shaven, dressed in Eastern outing clothes of dignified correctness. He put on a pair of glasses to peer closer at the two who came in hand in hand like adventuring children, with the lithe, half-fearful grace of wild things.

A tall and sallow man behind the counter smiled under his long, ragged, blond mustache and made a gesture of polite greeting.

"Well, you've sure kept us in the dark as to your movements, Peter Garth. We had no notion there was a bride in these parts until the sheriff brought us back word the other day. Ma'am, I'm glad to make your acquaintance." He glanced keenly and curiously at Sylvie's averted face.

"I'd have been here before," she said, "but I've been suffering from snow-blindness."

"Ah, that's bad sometimes. Your eyes are better now?"

"Y-yes, I think so."

"I can give you a first-class lotion, lady."

Sylvie and he discussed the lotion while Pete stood, drawn up, proud and silent, his cheeks flushed, waiting to dispose of his pelts. The bartering prolonged itself in spite of his best endeavors. Sylvie seemed to have no sense of peril or anxiety. She insisted upon taking a bite of early supper, forced coffee and bread and meat upon her companion, and chatted affably. Pete saw that the Eastern stranger had riveted upon her his attention, that he observed every gesture, listened to every word, and while she ate, that he walked over and asked a few murmured questions of the trader, nodding his head, then shaking it over the answers as though they confirmed some suspicion or anxiety.

At last Pete could bear the delay no longer. Gruffly he bade Sylvie come with him. He caught her hand and led her out, she looking back over her shoulder like a loath child. They had gone but a few yards along the beach trail when the sober, solid gentleman came out across the porch and waved his hand to them. Pete hastened his steps without replying. Then came a summons in a loud, full, authoritative voice: "Hi, there! One moment, please."

It was already evening; the lake was ruffled rosily under a sunset light. Pete stopped and turned. He waited, pale, tightlipped, and formidable; Sylvie moved a little closer to him. This mysterious summons gave her a first little spasm of distrust and fear. The man's square body and square, serious face bore down upon them, freighted with incongruous judgments. He came sturdily, defying the unspoken threat of loneliness.

He spoke when he came up to them—spoke with evident effort.

"My friends," he said, "I am a minister of the gospel, and though my mission in this wilderness does not rightly include you in its ministrations, still, my conscience, the commands of my Master, will not allow me to neglect so obvious and urgent a call for spiritual aid."

He cleared his throat. "Your name I didn't catch," he said doubtfully, and Pete did not supply the knowledge, "but I heard you introduce this young woman as your wife. I watched her very closely; I watched you, too, sir; I took the liberty of making some inquiries about you. I have had much and varied experience in the study of human nature." Here he put out a broad, clean hand with square finger-tips and lifted Sylvie's brown, unwilling left hand high from her side. "I am a minister of the gospel," he repeated. "In a land where such a symbol is thought much of, this woman has no wedding-ring. There is no register of your marriage here in the one spot where such a registration might have been most conveniently made—"

Sylvie jerked away her fingers; Pete laid down his load and slowly drew his right hand into a terrible fist.

"No, no!" The square-tipped fingers were lifted deprecatingly. "You must not be angry with me, my children. I am not here to judge you. I have no knowledge of your temptation, of your difficulties; you have met and loved in a wild and difficult land. I was not even sure of my surmise. Now, however; your silence and your anger confirm my opinion. I want only to offer you my services. Will you continue in your life and love as I have seen them to be, or will you, if only for the sake of other lives not yet your responsibility—perhaps, will you take advantage of this opportunity which God has now given you and let me make you indeed man and wife?"

Pete's fist was still terrible, and his lips were gathering their words, when Sylvie unbelievably spoke.

"Pete," she asked tremulously, and he felt her drawing even closer to his side, "Pete, don't you want—you *do* want—I know—I mean, will you, would you—marry me?"

He was dumb as a rock, and gray. His hand opened; he stared from her to the impossible intruder, the worker of the miracle, or rather for he felt like a beast trapped, the strange layer of the snare. For an instant the lake and the forest and the red sky turned in a great wheel before his eyes. Then he caught Sylvie's wrist almost brutally in his hand. "Be quiet!" he said; it was the savage speaking to his woman. "You've gone mad. Come with me. As for you, sir, my marrying or not marrying is none of your business—"

The minister looked sadly up into the young man's white and rigid face.

"God be with you!"

He bowed, turned and walked back along the beach, hands locked behind his broad tweed back, his head bent.

Pete tightened his grip on Sylvie's arm. "Come," he said to her as harshly as before. "We must hurry. It's nearly night."

Sylvie set her small teeth tight, bent down her head, and followed him without a word. Their silence seemed to grow into a pressure, a weight. It bent Pete's shoulders and Sylvie's slender neck, and whitened their lips. All that they did not dare to say aloud bulked itself, huge and thunderous, before the combined consciousness which makes a strange third companion in such dual silences. They dared not pause, or look at each other, or move their strained lips for fear truth, the desperate, treacherous truth, would leap out and link them like a lightning-flash. The somber forest enveloped them. They moved through it as through a deep wall that opened by enchantment. The moon came up, gibbous and white and glittering, paler than silver; and the forest became streaked and mottled with its light. A soft, sudden wind tore the light and shade into eerie, dancing ribbons and tatters and shreds. There were such sounds as are not heard in daylight—moon sounds and cloud sounds and sounds of dark wind; branches talked and other small voices answered in anxious undertones. A moose rubbed his antlers and coughed. They heard his big body hulking through a swamp down there in a well of darkness.

"I can't go so fast." Sylvie's shaken voice moved doubtfully. "I'm tired."

She pulled at his arm and stopped. The whole forest seemed to sway and stir and urge them to haste and secrecy.

"A storm's coming," Pete answered. "I can't carry you, Sylvie, unless I leave my load."

"Do you think I'd let you carry me?" she answered through her set teeth. "I'd rather die here than let you lift me up in your arms. I'll go on till I drop. I don't care for the storm. But I can't walk so fast. How can you see? The moon isn't—can't be, I mean—very, very bright here in the woods."

"The moon? There's a big storm-cloud just going to wipe it out. Listen! Don't you hear that thunder, that wind?"

The storm blew its distant trumpets, shouted louder, trampled the world with great steps, crashed and came upon them with a wet, cold blast. They were stunned with noise, dazzled with flashes, smothered and beaten with long, wet whips. Under a big rocking pine which shouted with a hundred confused tongues they found a dangerous shelter. Not far from them a tree was struck, splitting their ears, half stunning them. When the worst was over, Pete drew Sylvie out relentlessly and started in the heavily falling rain. The storm was drawing away, but the night was still impenetrably black. They walked for a few groping yards when Pete gave a sudden desperate laugh and stopped.

"What's the good of this! We're off the trail. We'll have to wait for the light. My God! How cold and wet and trembling you are." He threw down his pack, took off his coat, wet only on the outside, and wrapped it closely about her. She felt that he parted branches for her, and she knew that they were in a dry, still, scented place whose walls stirred and breathed. She sank down beside him on the smooth pine-needles and crept close. They were giddy, beaten and confused; they felt each other's trembling warmth; for greater comfort she tucked her hands under his arm. Her head dropped back against his shoulder so that her breath fell on his cheek. He felt the silent tears of her humiliation, hot and bitter and human after the cold, impersonal wetness of rain. It was as though a hand drew them together in the darkness; they moved numbly at the same instant, by the same impulse; then with a sort of convulsion they were in each other's arms. Cold, wet, tremulous, their lips met. The night became the beating of a heart.

CHAPTER XIV

Hugh sat in his great carved chair, his hands laid out across the bulky arms, his head bent forward a little so that his eyes encompassed all the restless beauty of the fire. After nightfall, when the wind began to shake the cabin, he had built up the fire, and its light now fought ruddily against the whiteness of the moon. Hugh had not lighted his lamp, nor let Bella light it, but he told her to make some strong coffee and keep it hot on the stove. "When Sylvie comes in," he had said, "she'll be exhausted. We'll give her a hot drink and send her to bed, eh, Bella! The foolish child!" This had been said softly, but with a wild, half-vacant look which Bella could not meet.

It was her belief that Pete and Sylvie had gone, not to return that night or any other night. In a desperate, still fashion she guarded this flaming conviction, peering up from long contemplations of it to learn whether there flickered any light of torment on Hugh's face. But all day, after the queer blankness of face and eyes with which he had first received her news of Sylvie's disappearance, he had been alternately gay and tranquil. All morning he had mended his boat, and in the afternoon he had cleaned his gun; and whenever he could cajole Bella into being his audience, he had talked. His talk was all of Sylvie, of her pretty childishness, her sweet, wayward ways, of her shyness, her timidity; and later, when supper was cleared away and he had throned himself in the center of that familiar circle of firelight, he had dropped his beautiful voice to a lower key and had boasted of Sylvie's love for him.

Bella sat on a big log sawed to the height of a low stool. She sat with her face bent down between her hands as though she were saving her eyes from the fire, but those bright, devoted eyes never left Hugh's face, though sometimes they made of it but a blurred image set in the broken crystals of her tears.

Thus, together, they heard the first rumble of the storm and saw the white squares of moonlight wiped from the floor as with a dark cloth. Next, the windows seemed to jump at them and jump away. "Lightning!" said Hugh. "She'll be afraid! Will Pete be able to comfort her? Will he, Bella?" Then, because she took courage to look into his face, she saw that his heart had been burnt all day, but that his faith, stronger than his fear, had kept the flame smothered, almost below his consciousness.

While the storm raged across their roof, beat a brutal tattoo close above their deafened heads, pushed at the door, drove a pool of water under the threshold, Hugh walked up and down, to and fro, from fire to window, from door to wall, but not fast, rather with a sort of stateliness. Sometimes he looked sidelong at Bella's expressionless, listening face. At last he forced himself back to the chair and sat there, mechanically polishing the barrel of his gun, but his tongue still spoke the saga of illusion. It stopped when the storm dropped into the bottomless silence of dawn. Then there was only the dripping from their eaves. Hugh sat there, very white, his gun laid across his lap. Bella, as white, lifted her face.

"They're coming," she whispered, and got stiffly to her feet.

Hugh moved back into his chair, turning sidewise and gathering himself as though for a spring. His nervous hands clutched at his gun. Upon the silence the door opened, and Pete and Sylvie came into the room. Wet and storm-beaten and beautiful they were, with scarlet cheeks.

Pete came quickly over to Hugh's chair; he let fall his pack and gazed resolutely down at his brother's face.

"Sylvie had a fancy to come with me to the trading-station," he said. "She came out after me and didn't overtake me until just where the trail comes out into the road. We hurried back, but the storm caught us. It was pitch-black in the woods; we couldn't keep the trail. We had to wait for daylight. I hope you weren't too anxious about her, Hugh.—Bella"—he glanced over his shoulder—"could you make us some hot coffee and help Sylvie into some dry clothes? We are properly drenched, both of us."

This speaker of terse, authoritative sentences was not the boy that had gone out that morning. That boy was gone forever.

Hugh stood up and looked slowly from Sylvie, who had stayed near the door and held her head up like a queen, to Pete.

"Where were you," he asked gently—"where were you while it stormed?"

Pete moved toward the fire, holding out his hands. "Ugh!" he shivered, "I'm numb with cold."

"Where were you," Hugh repeated, "during the storm?"

Pete lifted his eyes slowly. They were bluer than the blue heart of a sapphire. "Under a pine-tree," he answered casually enough, and then, just as Hugh would have smiled, the color creeping up into his lips, Pete's young and honest blood poured over his forehead, engulfing him, blazing the truth across his face. Bella saw it and clenched her hands. Sylvie's cheeks, too, caught fire. Hugh turned from him, blinded by terror, saw Sylvie's trembling mouth in her dyed countenance, and turned back. He lifted the hand that had held, all this while, to the chair, and balled it into a fist.

"Don't strike him," said Sylvie quietly, not moving from her place by the door. "Don't ever strike him again—*Ham Rutherford!*"

Hugh's bones seemed to crumble; his knees bent; he leaned back against the chair, holding to it behind him with both hands. The gun clattered to the floor. In the silence Sylvie walked across the room and lifted her face. As if for the first time they saw her eyes, black and brilliant and young, sharpening the softness of her features. She looked at Hugh mercilessly, pitilessly.

"I've been able to see you for a long time now, Ham Rutherford," she said. "And the instant I first saw you, I knew your name. Ever since the night you told me that story about the river, I've been watching you. You are a great and infamous liar! Yes, I know that you once killed a man for telling you that. Kill me if you like, for I am going to repeat it after him—a liar, hideous and deformed outside and in. I have no pity for a liar. Not even your physical misfortune shall shield you! You have made too great a mockery of it. You brought me here, blind, as helpless as one of the things you catch in your traps, and you played the hero with me. And you fed me with lies and lies and lies. I've eaten and drunk them until I'm sick. Now stand up and look at the truth. You are to eat that until *you* are sick.—No, Bella; no, Pete; I'm going to speak; no one can stop me. I know you love him. How you can look at him and see him as he is and know what he has done and still love him, I can't understand. Now, Hugh Garth—the name you tried to make me love you by—I'll tell these people that love you, some of the beautiful fables with which you tried to win *my* love. Maybe, then, they will begin to see you as you are. Here is the first: 'There was once a very noble youth who had a friend—'"

"Don't!" Hugh groaned pitifully, his head bent before her.

"Perhaps I won't; after all, it's not interesting unless you're fool enough, or blind enough, to be tricked into fancying it's the truth. But let me tell them some of the other things. This noble youth, this man sacrificed his life for his friend and bore the blame of that friend's guilt. He is as handsome as a Viking, the very ideal of a girl's imagination, strong and shapely and graceful. Has he a humped shoulder and a lame leg and a scarred face revealing his scarred soul? Answer me."

Hugh flinched as though under a lash.

Pete put out his hand uncertainly; his face was drawn with pain. "Sylvie—stop. You *must* stop. You're too cruel. He did lie to you, but remember, that was because he—"

The brilliant black eyes flashed back at him.

"Because he loved me, you were going to say? When you love a woman, do you try to ruin her life? Do you creep up in the dark under cover of her blindness and touch her with some dreadful, poisonous wound? You don't know my horror of that man, Pete. Oh, he kissed—kissed me!" She shivered. "A murderer! Yes, a murderer. Oh, Ham Rutherford, if I could only *make* you see yourself! If I could give you my eyes when they opened, and I saw Pete's beauty and Bella's sweetness and the horrible ugliness of you! And then, day by day—you see, I was afraid to let you know that I *had* seen you. I was in terror of you, of what you might do to me. I was afraid of you all; you had all deceived me. Day by day I learned the utter distortion of you, mind, body, and soul. How could I help but—but—" She faltered and half turned to Pete, holding out her hands. Her indignation at the treachery practiced upon her, an anger that had grown in silence to unbearable heat, had spent itself in words. She was all for consolation now—for sympathy. But Pete stepped back from her. He was looking at Hugh, and his clear, young face was an open wound.

Hugh pushed himself up and slowly lifted his face. It was then that he saw Sylvie's hands stretched out to Pete. He started—no one knew what the convulsive movement meant; but as he started—the gun tripped him. He caught it up carelessly, blindly. There was a flash—a crash. Pete leaped and bent, holding his arm. Blood spurted between his fingers, soaking his wet sleeve; and Sylvie, crying aloud, wrapped him in trembling, protective arms.

"I'm not much hurt," he said half dazedly. "It—it was an accident. He didn't mean it. I was looking at him. The gun went off. He didn't shoot at me.... *Hugh!*"

The man was staring straight ahead of him, and now he drew his hand across his eyes, the fingers crooked as though they tore a veil.

"Now," he said, "I do see myself just as I am. Yes, I did shoot at you. Yes, I think I meant to kill you. I must have meant to kill you. That's the truth. For the second time I'm a murderer. Yet now, as God lives, even if I am down in the dust, I'll lay hold of my stars. I'm going to walk out of your lives so that they can shape themselves to their own good ends. Sylvie can shape yours with you, Pete." He hesitated a moment. "If a coward, a murderer, can say 'God bless you,' take that blessing!"

He picked up his gun and shuffled across the floor, flinching aside from Bella as though he could bear no further touch or word, and went out of the door, letting in the brightness of the sunrise.

Pete had sunk into a chair, faint from the shock and weakness of his wound; and Sylvie bent over him. For a minute, in great and bitter loneliness Bella stood and watched them; then she followed Hugh.

He had put down his gun and gone slowly up from the hollow and was walking along the river-bank. He had the look of a man who strolls in meditation. When he came to his boat where it lay near the roots of the three big pines, he turned it over—he had been mending its bottom the morning of yesterday—and began to push it down toward the plunging stream. The glitter of morning took all the swirlings and ripplings and plungings of the swift water in its golden hands. Hugh steadied the boat. Above him on the bank Bella spoke quietly.

"Hugh," she said, "look up at me. What are you going to do?"

He lifted his face, still holding to the boat.

"What are you going to do?" she repeated.

"Why do you want to know? You've heard the truth."

She came down the bank and stood beside him so close that her hair, loosened by the wind, was blown against his shoulder. She pressed it back and gazed into his eyes. The inner glow had worn through at last. She was all warmth, all flame now. She smiled with soft and parted lips. "Do you think that was the truth of you, my dear," she said, "*my* truth of you? I have always seen you as you are. But"—she drew a big breath, like a climber who has reached the height—"but—I came to you, didn't I?"

Hugh's eyes widened, the pupils swallowing her light. "You—you came to me? Not for Pete's sake?"

"Never for his sake."

"But, Bella—you laughed at me."

"Yes, once, for your poor folly in trying to be what you are not. When have I ever laughed at what you are? It's what you are I've loved, my dear, just what you are—a tormented child. Only be honest with me, Hugh. Tell me what do you want: the moon now or—or all the truth?"

"I want the truth—and the end," he said. "I'm going down the river."

She glanced at the flood as though it were a brook. "I am going with you then. You must take me. My life has always been yours."

He laid one of his hands on either of her cheeks so that her face was framed for him to read. It was flushed; the deep eyes were beautiful.

"You—all these empty years! *You*, Bella." It was as though he saw her now for the first time. The revelation dazzled him. "I've gone thirsty, with wine at my elbow, until it's too late." He shook his shoulders. "Come with me, then, if you must."

She stepped into the boat and sat in the stern, her hands folded in her lap, her eyes in their great and sudden beauty still fixed on his face. The wind blew her hair wildly in a long, streaming veil across her forehead, down her cheek, out over her shoulder. She was beautiful with the joy that was hers at last.

Hugh stepped in and stood to push the boat out from the shore. His eyes never left hers. It was a deep, long look of which her soul drank, quenching its thirst. Very slowly the boat moved; then it turned. A hand seemed to grip it's prow. There was a mighty, confused roaring in their ears; the bank seemed to be snatched back from them. The sunlight, shone into Hugh's face. Suddenly he caught at his oar.

"The river is not so high," he shouted; "the flood's going down." He looked away from her and back. "We have—just a chance. We'll leave it to the river. It may be the end of you and me—or, Bella, it may be the beginning."

He steadied the boat with all his skill. It was drawn with frightful swiftness down the swollen stream.

Before noon Sylvie and Pete moved slowly across the open space and went back along their forest trail. They walked like lovers, and Sylvie's arm helped to support him. Just before he stepped in among the trees he turned for a long, desolate, backward look.

Now the hoop of green, once white as paper under the noon sun, and the level, circular rim of the forest are empty and silent except for the rattling of the river and the moving of the pines against the fixed, grave stars. The human tragedy—or was it comedy?—has burnt itself out like the embers of a camp-fire that will never again be kindled in that lonely spot.

THE END

Milton Keynes UK
Ingram Content Group UK Ltd.
UKHW011124180424
441376UK00004B/206